Cat Ladies

Amanda Armstrong and Christina St. Clair

Published by Rogue Phoenix Press, LLP
Copyright © by Amanda Armstrong and Christina St. Clair
All Rights Reserved

ISBN: 978-1-62420-872-0

Cover Art: Designs by Ms G
Editor: C. L. Kraemer

Dedication

To Mum
Precious and warm a memory; I still can see Blue Velvet.

*"A cat will stay loyal as long as you are,
disrespect a cat, you disrespect yourself."* – Anonymous

Prologue

Victoria

Victoria was not looking forward to this evening. In fact, she was dreading it. It was a meeting of minds, apparently. Basically, five women in their late fifties, getting together for wine and chat. To talk about books. It was never about books though. It was all about gossip and whose marriage had been the worst. Victoria knew the answer to that, but it wasn't her story to tell. Her ginger shorthair cat, Biscuit, a stray she'd taken in, rubbed against her legs. "Good girl," she said, patting her head. "I would rather stay home with you, but I promised Charlotte I'd come tonight and maybe I can get them to talk intelligently about the book we're supposed to have read."

Charlotte

Charlotte wiped the already spotless glasses and set them on the counter, ready for the ladies to come and drink her wine and pretend to talk about literature. Yet she knew, as soon as she went out of her beautiful designer-grey living room to fetch the snacks, they'd point to the wedding photos lined up on the marble fireplace mantlepiece and speculate about what had happened to her marriage. "Darling Mirabelle," she murmured to her long-haired Persian, "it's a good thing I love you." She picked up some strands of fur and wondered if she ought to run the vacuum again. She certainly didn't want the other women to criticize her housekeeping skills. Mirabelle meowed for food, and Charlotte rushed into the kitchen to replenish her kibble bowl.

Lizzie

Lizzie, who lived across the green in a tiny cottage, all she could afford to rent—sighed as she put on her coat. "Here we go, another night with the heathens." She smiled wryly as she spoke the words out loud and went over to her dresser. Give me strength, she thought, gazing at the 'Home is Where the Heart is!' plaque her ex had given her before he'd left her high and dry. She picked up her keys from the dark wooden dresser that she'd wanted to replace years ago but…yeah, well. Tom, her sweet lame kitty, went on grooming his paws, but as she left the house, he lifted his head and watched her departure through his slit green eyes. "Bye," she mouthed into the silent house.

Cathy

Cathy, who'd lived in the village for many years, stared into the mirror, hating what she saw: crepey arms and neck, a menopausal belly purse hanging over her crotch. "What's even the point of me?" she muttered under her breath before fluttering a hand up in front of her face. She pulled on some too-tight jeans hoping they'd make her belly look flatter. The tunic top she selected covered her bulging waistline. After smearing on more concealer over the red spots from her rosacea, she got out a silk scarf and waved it at Molly, her blue grey, but the cat wasn't interested, curled up on the bed, taking a nap.

Lou

Lou smiled at herself in the mirror. "Looking good, Doll!" She swiped the bright red lipstick from her front teeth with a perfectly manicured finger and twirled around. She was so glad she'd moved to this small village, Ickenham, where she felt important, unlike being one of too many wannabes in London. Over the years, she'd gotten a few roles in TV commercials, but nothing big ever came her way. She enjoyed book talk with the girls, knowing her career as an actress impressed them. Tonight was going to be her star performance. For, tonight was the night, she was going to tell them about the leading role she'd just landed, and she wanted to look the part. Peregrine, the Manx cat, who was as special as his mistress, purred. "It's at times like this I wish I had a tail to wag." His eyes, full of love, met Lou's.

Chapter One

Charlotte

Charlotte drank a glass of wine to try to calm her nerves before the ladies arrived. This was the fifth meeting of their newly started book club, and she was the last to host. She was always anxious about people coming over, afraid she wouldn't be good enough and she'd upset them in some way. She'd always been shy and socially inept around people. She'd rather be on her own and not face anyone. As she sipped her chardonnay, sitting in her lounge, she could see the rain streaming down her front windows. It was teeming down. She hoped it wouldn't be a problem for the women to get here. On the other hand, if no one came, it would be a relief.

This awful rain reminded her of the first time she met her ex-husband, John. He'd been so sweet to her when she'd begun studying at the University of Pittsburgh, overwhelmed by so many buildings scattered everywhere. Parking had been a nightmare on that first day. She probably would easily have found the Cathedral of Learning, the forty-two-story gothic building, but she was terrified about trying to locate her classroom. A tall fellow in blue jeans came across the road, wielding a large umbrella, and when he saw her getting out of her car, he held it aloft to shelter her and led her to her room. He'd been a professor. How could she not fall for this sexy man with his Georgia drawl? They'd married while she was still a sophomore.

After ten years, and a son and daughter later, who were now grown up, she realised that she'd leaned on him too much. She never understood, or perhaps refused to believe, his late nights and excuses for having to go away on weekends were not about lectures but about other women. And there hadn't only been one. What was really stupid was that he had divorced her! As if she'd been the one who was unfaithful. She'd been devastated and swore she'd never date or remarry.

Several years as a single mother took up all of her energy and time. But a guy with an accent, Colin, a visiting marine biologist at the college where she was a professor, swept her off her feet. He was English. Classy. Taller than her (almost) six feet frame and charming. He was promoting his book about how crabs were misused and bled to provide a special chemical used in vaccines. There was now a synthetic chemical that was cheaper and more efficient that ought to put a stop to this practice. She'd only gone to the lecture for something to do but his presentation had impressed her. Afterwards, she'd attended the reception. She'd thought herself beyond romance and unattractive to men, but he'd grabbed her hands and smiled into her eyes and asked her to dinner the following day. She'd never regretted going and before she knew it, she'd agreed to move to England with him. Her kids were grown, and there seemed nothing to keep her in the States. London was a dream come true, the country of Shakespeare, Austen, and Rowling. In fact, she'd recommended *Pride and Prejudice* for their first book, but Lou had groaned, and they'd all agreed to read *Fifty Shades of Gray*. How ridiculous, she'd thought, but went along with them, hoping she might yet introduce them to some literature.

She glanced up at the photo of her and Colin on their wedding day and sighed deeply. Where had he gone? Even though she'd called in a missing person report to the police, they had not found him. It had been three years. He'd so often gone on deep sea missions and might or might not still be alive. She'd told her lady friends that she was divorced, and that was true, but she had no intention of telling them about her second husband, Colin's, disappearance.

Mirabelle jumped onto the sill of the deep bay window and stretched out, purring, but when a cab pulled in front of the house and out leaped Lou in leopard skin tights beneath a bright orange tunic, the cat made a hasty retreat up the stairs.

Lou flung open a huge yellow and green umbrella, perhaps intending to be glamorous, but only succeeding in looking flamboyant, so unlike her serious and brilliant Colin. Lou had made sure in their first get-together that everyone knew she was an important actress. Charlotte doubted it was true but didn't challenge her. It would be unkind, and she hated confrontation. Even her students knew she was a pushover. She never gave even the worst of students a failing grade.

As Lou came wobbling down the front path on her wedged shoes, Charlotte hurried to the front door and pushed it open, moving to one side to let Lou through. "Oh, sorry," Lou said with a big smile as she dropped her umbrella on the tile floor. "It's dripping everywhere."

Charlotte resisted running to get a mop. "Glad to see you," she said quietly, wanting to tell Lou to remove her shoes before going into the living room, but of course she did not. It might be insulting to her guest, not that pushy Lou would care.

"Wow! A white rug! Are you crazy?" Lou strode across to one of the linen pushback recliners, plonked down and kicked off her shoes that had left wet spots across the carpet. "That's better," she muttered, obviously intending to make herself at home, which of course Charlotte hoped for, but not at the expense of her spotless house. She managed a wry smile and wondered why Lou didn't have the book with her.

The doorbell rang so Charlotte excused herself to let in the next of the ladies. Victoria and Lizzie crowded into the entry hall, stepping around the overly large brolly. "I bet I know who brought that," Victoria said, taking off a tan raincoat and hanging it on the coat stand. Lizzie took off her tatty navy peacoat and put it on the hook next to Victoria's. They both had on jeans and tee-shirts causing Charlotte to feel overdressed in her pleated skirt that she thought was English-looking and would help her fit in. Even her Marks and Spencer's matching blouse seemed ridiculous. Next to these two, she felt like a school ma'am, which of course she was. Next to Lou, she'd felt like an old prude, which she wasn't. After all, she'd had two husbands and remembered some amazing sex that the stupid book they were reading had reminded her she missed.

Chapter Two

Lou

Lou hadn't missed the muttered snide remark about her umbrella by Victoria as she'd arrived, and she rolled her eyes. *Screw you*, she thought, *you're just jealous, you old prune*. She chuckled to herself and looked around the immaculate living room. Well, formerly immaculate, she noted, her eyes glancing at the dirty wet prints her shoes had left on the carpet upon her arrival.

It had given her a thrill to watch Charlotte itching to clean it up, but desperate to give off some kind of nonchalance. *Ha! You don't fool me, Miss Prim and Proper.*

"Hey ladies," she beamed as Charlotte ushered Victoria and Lizzie into the room, rising up from her seated position to air kiss the other women.

"How are you, Lou?" Lizzie, her shoulders always hunched as though the weight of the world resided on them, gingerly offered a cheek.

"I'm ready for vino and getting down and dirty with Mr Gray, is how I am!" She cackled, finding amusement in the blush that spread across Lizzie's face, and the utter disdain on Victoria's.

"Yes, of course," Charlotte fussed, "drinks? Chardonnay for everyone?"

A chorus of affirmatives chimed up and Charlotte hurried from the room.

"Where's your copy of the book then, Lou?" Victoria eyed the other woman's empty hands, raising an over plucked eyebrow that made her look constantly startled.

"Doll, I don't need notes; I got it all up here!" Lou prodded her skull with a long, manicured talon and then clutched her well-endowed chest as she giggled coquettishly.

Victoria gave a loud tut, but Lou didn't miss the tiniest of smirks on Lizzie's face.

"Mind you," Lou continued, encouraged by Lizzie's mirth, "I'm not sure what in my head is of the fictional Mr. Gray or of my own actual memories!"

"Lou, shame on you!" Victoria snorted and shook her head, just as Charlotte re-entered the room with a tray of glasses.

As the girls made small talk, Lou thought back to her last comment.

Despite her bragging about her sexual encounters, this wasn't strictly the case. Yes, she'd had some fabulous sex over the years, but honestly, the mind-blowing kind she bragged of were only ever with one person. On and off, over almost three decades, she and her lover had met in clandestine hotels all over the world. Never for long, and never enough, but hers all the same. Until he would have to return to his wife and family, and she, to her failed auditions for walk on TV parts and a world of rejection and of fear that as her looks faded, so would her spirit and any hope of success. She glanced down at her bright, sassy outfit, knowing the other girls thought her too brash and too brassy, but determined that she would never let her colours fade. With a sinking heart she wondered if it was too late; she hadn't heard from her lover in over three months now and feared that his interest had waned as quickly as it had begun.

Twenty-eight years ago, she, a young beautiful twenty-seven-year-old theatre actress at the after-show party in the Wimbledon theatre, had almost ran straight into the arms of Richard. He, ten years her senior, his dark hair with only a smattering of grey, dark eyes framed by thick lashes, wearing a navy Savile Row suit, had been standing at the bar, a drink in his right hand, and a gleaming band of gold on his left.

She should have walked away then: That gold wedding band screaming at her to back off. Unfortunately, his eyes upon her body, taking in her tight corset top and long slinky satin skirt, screamed at her that he would more than please her if she so chose.

And so, she did. And so began almost thirty years of loneliness, pain, jealousy, and guilt. Through all of this she consoled herself with other lovers, another life: the glamourous, aspiring actress, free and fun loving; the good time girl. But she was always waiting for the call, the command, from him, from wherever he was in the world. But recently, no command had come, and that stung.

Chin up, Doll! She inwardly sighed. *You're an actress, you can style it out.*

And yes, she thought smugly, *my new role will prove that.* She puffed out her chest and threw her head back dramatically. "Ladies," she announced grandly, "I have some news!"

Before she could continue, the doorbell rang, announcing the arrival of Cathy.

As Charlotte scurried to the front door, Lou side-eyed Victoria who was watching her with an expectant look on her thin face.

"I'll tell you when we're all here." Lou winked at her, then threw back a gulp of wine as she waited for the group to gather.

Chapter Three

Victoria

"I'm sorry I'm late," Cathy told the group, following Charlotte into the lounge. "I could use a glass of wine after my morning."

"Oh dear," Charlotte said sympathetically. "You sit on the couch, and I'll pour you a large chardonnay."

"What's going on?" Victoria asked, noticing that Cathy looked more down in the dumps than usual.

Her tight blue jeans did nothing to hide her middle age spread. *My goodness, why did women make such fools of themselves?* she thought.

Cathy took her wine from Charlotte and held it up for a toast. "Here's to positive medical results!" she said, almost in tears.

"What?" Lizzie said, and they all looked at one another and back at Cathy.

"I had to have a biopsy. Ovarian. The doctor said my blood tests are a little high but probably not cancer. We have to wait for the lab results."

"I used to work in the lab at St. Thomas. I can use my contacts to try and get your lab results faster," Victoria offered.

"I have no idea where the test will be done," Cathy lamented.

Charlotte sank onto the couch next to her, wanting to give her a reassuring hug, but the sound of the door opening made her and everyone else look up expectantly at the entrance to the room. "Who on earth could that be?" Charlotte felt twitters in her tummy as heavy footsteps sounded, coming towards them.

A tall man with dark hair greying at the temples, wearing a tweed coat, stood in the doorway. "Oh! I thought you'd be alone, Charlotte!" he muttered, his voice a little strained.

"What are you doing here?" Charlotte cried.

Before he had a chance to answer, Victoria leapt to her feet. "Get out!" Her eyes stormy, she plucked her cell phone out of her pocket. "I'm calling the police!"

"Wait!" the man said. "Tell them who I am, Charlotte."

Charlotte's shoulders slumped. "He is my ex-husband. I don't want him here!"

"Get out, *you, you* stalker!" Victoria yelled, striding towards the guy, who backed up.

"I'll be in touch later, Charlotte." He made a hasty retreat, and they soon heard the door slam behind him.

"I am so sorry girls," Charlotte murmured, watching him through the window, heading down the street that led to Ickenham Tube Station. "I have no idea what he could possibly want. We've been divorced for years."

Victoria sidled over to the mantelpiece and picked up the photo of Colin. "So, who is this chap?" she asked.

Charlotte's face turned bright red. "I can't talk about it right now. Let's talk about the first chapters in the book, the ones we were supposed to all have read. Who wants to start?"

There was silence in the room for several moments. "We're not your students," Lou said, glaring at Charlotte and then laughing. "I'd rather talk about our sex lives!"

Everyone looked embarrassed. Charlotte straightened her skirt. Cathy fidgeted with her tunic top. Lizzie stared into space. Victoria turned and faced Lou, looming over her. "My sex life is none of your business!" she yelled.

Lou grinned. "I say we tell of our first kiss and the first in and out with a guy," she said rudely. "Come on," she coaxed. "We're all adults here. Unless for some of you it was so long ago, you can't remember!"

Victoria clenched her fists as if she might whack Lou, but Charlotte quickly deflected. "Let me get the snacks. I have mini quiches and other nibbles."

Victoria offered her hand to Lizzie who let herself be pulled up from her chair. "We're leaving," she said.

Lizzie nodded and smiled sadly at Charlotte. "I'm sorry," she said. "I'll host next week, if you like."

No one responded as the two departed.

Outside, once they were no longer within sight of the house, Victoria gripped Lizzie's hand. "I cannot *stand* that Lou! And what's with Charlotte's man on the mantel. Is he a lover, do you think? Or an old boyfriend?"

"I have no idea," Lizzie responded, "But Charlotte's grown-up kids all had dark hair and looked like the intruder. Two-timing bastards make me so angry," she ranted.

"I know." Victoria swung Lizzie towards her and hugged her. "You've got me now!"

Chapter Four

Cathy

Cathy felt her heart go out to shy, retiring Charlotte; she knew these evenings were difficult for her. Hosting it herself would have felt like an enormous task, but to then have her ex-husband show up. Wow, she must feel mortified.

"What is with those two?" Lou asked incredulously as Charlotte simply gazed at her hands in her lap.

"Are you okay?" Cathy gently asked Charlotte, deliberately ignoring Lou's comment.

"Yes, yes, of course, absolutely," Charlotte flustered, and Cathy noticed the smirk on Lou's face that she did nothing to disguise. Typical drama queen, loving the drama, she thought angrily.

"Would you like us to leave?" She made to stand up, but Charlotte was shaking her head.

"No, it's fine, let's carry on…"

"We can't without the other two, there's no point." Lou interrupted. "I mean, there's no point in discussing the book without them," she clarified.

Cathy saw Charlotte's shoulders visibly relax at the thought that her ruined evening was almost over. She was relieved; she wasn't in the mood for it tonight.

"However," Lou continued, with a wicked grin on her face, at which Cathy's heart sank. "There's still vino to be quaffed, and mini quiche to scoff, and perhaps some gossip to share?"

Cathy raised a wary eyebrow at her. "Gossip?"

Charlotte audibly sighed as Lou went on.

"Yes, don't you think those two," she eyed the front door, from where Lizzie and Victoria had recently departed, "are a little bit closer than just friends?" She drew quotation marks in the air with her fingers as she watched the other two.

Cathy narrowed her eyes. "What on Earth are you implying?"

Charlotte, wringing her hands in her lap, reddened, her eyes widening as she waited for Lou to respond.

Lou smiled and waggled her eyebrows suggestively. "You know, Lesbo's, dykes, gay…"

Charlotte looked horrified and jumped up from her seat. "I'm sorry, I really don't think such talk is right. Perhaps we can…"

Cathy quickly stood and caught Charlotte's arm, realising that as an academic known for tolerance, she must be appalled at Lou's insensitivity. "Take it easy, sit back down. We'll leave you be. You've had a terrible shock tonight." She guided Charlotte back to the sofa and eased her gently down.

"But…" Lou was open-mouthed as she began to protest, and had Cathy not been so concerned about Charlotte she would have probably laughed at her hang-dog impression.

"No, Lou," Cathy spoke firmly to shut her up, something she knew for certain Lou was not used to. "Enough for tonight, the last thing Charlotte needs to hear is your ridiculous gossip. She's had a terrible shock and…"

"But…" Lou repeated, and Cathy held up her hands to halt her.

"Enough." She repeated, as she bade goodbye to Charlotte with a promise to call her in a few days, gave a curt nod to Lou, whose return scowl almost made her chuckle, and walked out the front door.

Phew! She thought to herself once she was on the street. *Where the heck did I get that assertiveness from?* She shook her head, astounded at her bravery. She'd never been one to speak out; had spent most of her life quietly doing everyone's bidding without question, the thought of doing anything to put the spotlight on herself was her worst nightmare.

She'd been so needy when she'd started nursing, falling for the doctor who'd hurt and rejected her so cruelly. She'd run away from that hospital where she loved working like a scared rabbit and always regretted how she'd never worked as a proper nurse again. But at least today she had taken care of Charlotte and was proud of herself for being caring. Not to mention managing to be independent for years without anyone to prop her up or tell her what to do.

That horrible doctor had impressed her and had so easily been able to weave his way into her life, making her feel grateful for any attention he gave her. Gosh, she'd had a lucky escape from him if truth be known. He'd put her down when he thought she might be getting a 'bit too big for her boots', complimenting her when she was at her lowest, so that the immediate high of his rare kind words became addictive. And she had not noticed the subtle changes, the withholding of money, the passive aggressive comments, the eventual loss of her independence.

An independence that, even now, she struggled to find, despite the doctor being long gone. His soul-destroying intimidating control had left its mark, and she was still searching for herself, for who she was supposed to be. She wondered now if her current health issue was brought on by the stresses in her life, or was it something she'd done in her past? Had that man given her some sexual disease that led to the scare she was now facing?

She should stop over-fretting about it, she thought rationally, at least until she had the test results.

Cathy's stomach grumbled loudly, and she thought longingly of the mini quiches back at Charlotte's. She pinched the roll of her fat on her waist and felt her eyes sting with unshed tears.

Glancing up, she realised with surprise that she'd already arrived in the village, so lost in her thoughts she'd been. Her house was just a few minutes further over along the Ickenham Road, but as she waited for an oncoming car to pass before she could cross, she wrinkled her nose appreciatively. *Mmm,* she breathed deeply, inhaling the delicious food aromas coming from The White Bear pub.

She stood briefly in contemplation, then...

"Sod it," she muttered, "I'll start the diet tomorrow."

And with that, she turned and shuffled into the pub, thoughts of a crusty pie and crispy fries with gravy, the only thing on her mind.

Chapter Five

Charlotte

Charlotte tugged on her sneakers, which they called trainers here in England. She was wearing blue jeans and a flowery tunic that was a bit dressy, but that's all she had for this next session of the book club. She gripped her copy of "Fifty Shades" as she walked across the green to Lizzie's place. Thank goodness it wasn't raining. The old cottages where Lizzie lived had been gentrified and looked quite prosperous with their peaked roofs and brown brick facade, reminding her of posh townhouses back in Pittsburgh, reminding her too of John showing up unannounced. She'd ignored his many calls and deleted his text messages without reading them. That phase in her life was over. She did, of course, check with her son and daughter to make sure all was well with them. It was. She did not mention their father.

Victoria came to the door to let her into Lizzie's place. It flashed through Charlotte's mind that maybe there *was* something going on between the two women. But who cares! It was none of her business. She wished, in fact, that she had close friends the way these two took care of one another. She half-smiled to herself to think of Victoria running off her ex. But she hoped no one would question her because she had no answers that she cared to give anyone.

"Hi Charlotte!" Victoria smiled. "Cathy's already here. Come on into the kitchen and get yourself a glass of something and a plate. I thought we'd eat before we started our discussion. Lizzie and I put all the snacks on the counter."

Charlotte couldn't help but notice the place smelled of sausage rolls and a strong odor of dust, and the walls needed a coat of paint. The sofa she passed could use a cover or be completely replaced. Maybe she could offer

Lizzie her old one since she wanted to get something new, but maybe that would seem insulting.

Cathy was already in the kitchen carrying her Styrofoam plate loaded with sausage rolls, cucumber sandwiches, and scotch eggs. A large slice of cream gateaux sat on one side. The spread of food was not elegant, but it was plentiful, and it did look tasty. Charlotte helped herself to two cucumber sandwiches and took the glass of wine Lizzie offered her, following Cathy into the lounge to sit on the couch next to her. It was a good thing she hadn't worn black because cat hair was everywhere.

"We're all here except Lou," Victoria called from the kitchen. "If we're lucky, she won't show up!"

Cathy, looking sympathetic, met Charlotte's eyes, but Charlotte did not want to be catty about anyone, even though it had taken her two hours to clean the muddy marks from her rug and she'd cursed Lou's carelessness and, yes, perhaps even intentional thoughtlessness. Who knew what she might be dealing with in her life? She nibbled her sandwich and looked down.

Lizzie strolled into the living room carrying her cat. "This is Tom," she said. The cat jumped from her arms and limped over to Cathy, rubbing against her legs, obviously hoping for a treat. "Can I give him something?" she asked, reaching down to stroke the cat's back.

"Sure," Lizzie responded. "He loves sausage."

Everyone focused on Tom as he licked up a small piece of sausage roll and then made his rounds to each one of them. He turned his nose up at the cucumber but licked the butter from the bread Charlotte gave him. Eventually, he jumped on Victoria's lap. She petted him and he purred loudly. "My cat, Biscuit, was a stray like this one. He's a sweetheart too, very cuddly."

"I love cats," Cathy said. "My Molly came from animal rescue. She's a blue grey who my neighbour got, but after she got married, she couldn't keep her, so I took her and I'm glad I did."

"You may have glimpsed my Mirabelle last week," Charlotte said. "She's shy and doesn't make up with other people." She almost added that her kitty had loved her husband, the second one of course, but she wasn't about to say anything that might open up the conversation about her ex or her missing husband. They'd probably think she was foolish. "I wonder if Lou has a cat?"

"I pity any living creature that has to live with her," Victoria said and grinned. "Sorry girls, I promise not to be catty again."

They all laughed.

"We'd best get started then." Charlotte opened her book to the first chapter. "It's well written if you like this sort of thing," she said. "A complete imbalance of power between the college student and the good-looking entrepreneur."

"I kind of liked Christian," Cathy said, smirking. "I get that imbalance of power, but he's the kind of man women fall for. Love at first sight, or maybe lust is every girl's dream."

Victoria gave her a disapproving look and said, "All men are arseholes!"

"Not all men," Lizzie said meekly.

Victoria gasped, "You of all people must know better! Don't you agree, Charlotte?"

Charlotte felt her face turning bright red. Fortunately, before she had to say anything, Lizzie's phone chimed to the tune of Amazing Grace, of all things, which is exactly what she needed rather than talk about her sex life. Goodness, the first chapter only hinted at chemistry with moments of electricity, just like she'd felt with dear Colin. It made her want to cry with loneliness.

"It's Lou," Lizzie mouthed to them before hanging up. "She told me to turn on ITV2 and watch Love Island."

"Is this her idea of a joke?" Victoria said, frowning.

Chapter Six

Lou

As the beautiful, statuesque brunette strode towards her, Lou felt the butterflies in her stomach double down and she swallowed nervously.

"And so, I wanted to introduce the lovely Lou Gardener, who will be hosting the Love Island spin off for the more mature, single people: Second Chance Saloon!"

Lou smiled sweetly at Mara, itching to smack her face for the 'more mature' comment, but conceding that that was actually the case. She should be grateful, she knew, for this fantastic opportunity: her own show!

"Thanks, my darling," she enthused, crossing her tanned legs and adjusting her leopard print kaftan seductively, "and thanks for the welcome. I'm a huge fan!" she gushed.

"Bless you, and I think it's so great that people of your age want to find second chance love, it's so adorable!"

Could you be any more patronising?

"Well," Lou giggled coquettishly, "I think everyone deserves a second chance at love. We don't all have to settle for a solitary life with only a cat for company…"

"Hahaha hilarious, like a cat lady!" Mara's creamy pink mouth settled into a smirk before she continued. "And do you have a cat?"

Bitch!

"As a matter of fact, I do." Lou wasn't about to let this young upstart get to her. "Peregrine is the joy of my life; he's a Manx cat and he takes no prisoners. We are in fact rather similar like that, dear."

Shove that in your pipe and smoke it!

"How, erm, delightful… Now, shall we move on, what can we expect from Second Chance Saloon?"

Lou smiled inwardly, satisfied that the battle, although not quite victorious, was not lost either. As she began to explain the concept of the show she would be hosting from tomorrow, she imagined the book ladies all gawping in awe at the TV screen.

Haha, now they'll see my true star quality.

The show would originally feature eight over-fifty-year-olds, four men and four women, coming together in a country estate in Hertfordshire, all looking for love. There would be twists and turns and new people would arrive as original contestants left, and she, Lou Gardener would be overseeing it all.

It was a shame, she thought, that they weren't going to be filming in a more exotic location; a luxurious spacious Majorcan villa, but hey ho, at least she'd be near enough to the book ladies so that she could rub her success in their faces every once in a while, when she had a break from filming.

And who knew, maybe she could find her own Mr Gray with one of the male contestants, although she was certain that was way outside the boundaries of her role, but still...

Suddenly she had the wildest idea. What if she got to choose who enters the country house? What if she brought the book ladies in, one by one, her own little experiment?

She almost rubbed her hands in glee and laughed aloud at the thought of fat Cathy lolloping around a country house. Or mouse-like Charlotte, frightened to touch any of the antique artefacts for fear of breaking them. *What a hoot!* She'd definitely pitch it to her producer.

With the title credits rolling, Lou unhooked her mic and looked at Mara.

"Thank you, dear."

"No worries, good luck with your little show." Mara jumped up from her stool and without a backward glance stalked away, her long black hair whipping over her shoulders.

"Cow!" Lou muttered under her breath, "you'll get your just desserts, you mark my words."

She made her way to the catering car for a much-needed cold drink whilst she waited for her manager to arrive to take her to the airport, seething at the young woman.

What was it with the youth of today who treated anybody over the age of forty or so with such, well, not even contempt, it was just nothingness. As though once you hit thirty-six, you're invisible, useless, condemned to see out the remainder of your life in God's waiting room.

Well, not me. Life is for living, and boy am I going to live!

She thought again of the book ladies back home, she couldn't wait to hear what they thought about this!

Chapter Seven

Cathy

Cathy was glad to be hosting. It took her mind off the biopsy. She'd spent every day worrying, and whenever the post came, had held her breath, but when the official letter came, she'd stuck it under a pile of letters in the kitchen, unwilling to open it. She thought to call her doctor's office but couldn't bring herself to do that either. But now, at least, she could think of her guests. She'd prepared a plate of chicken salad sandwiches on pita bread, along with an assortment of biscuits, or cookies as Charlotte probably called them. She had bought them at a local bakery and had already tasted quite a few to make sure they were good. Right! She knew she was trying to comfort herself, but she deserved it and who cared if she was overweight? There was no man for whom she needed to keep herself trim for. What was the point?

There was a loud rap on her front door which she promptly answered, hoping it might be Charlotte who was always kind, but of course—just her luck it was Lou looking like a model; tall and willowy, especially in her *very* high heels, wearing tight leggings that showed off her shapely legs, and her tight sequined bodice revealing her well-endowed chest. "Hi, Lou, glad to see you," she lied, feeling dowdier than ever. "Come on in." She held the door open. "You're the first to arrive." She led Lou into her lounge, relieved it wasn't raining, and she wouldn't be faced with a muddy carpet to clean up. Not that she was a neatnik like Charlotte, but still, Lou was an insensitive bitch at times. And a gossip. "Beer or wine?" she asked.

Lou looked her up and down. "Wine, dear. I need to keep my figure trim. Especially now I'm hosting Second Chance Saloon."

Cathy resisted saying the ladies had watched Love Island and thought Lou looked haggard next to the black-haired vixen who'd introduced her. "Congratulations!" She managed to sound cheerful and was relieved when the other three women all arrived together, and she needed to busy herself settling them in.

Once they were all sitting with drinks in their hands, Victoria stared rudely at Lou. "Why don't you try dressing your age?" she uttered.

"She looks fine," Lizzie, who was sitting next to her on the sofa, moved a little further away.

Victoria turned her attention to Charlotte. "So, we were all wondering who the guy in the photo on your mantelpiece is because he doesn't even slightly resemble your children."

"It's none of our business," Cathy said, wanting to defend Charlotte, who looked as if she'd swallowed poison.

"It's okay." Charlotte regained her composure. "I'd rather talk about the book, but since you've asked. That is Colin, my second husband. The guy who you chased away, Victoria, was John, my first husband and the father of my children. I haven't had much to do with him for years."

"What did he want?" Lizzie chimed in. "I had to take out a restraining order on my ex. He was a real arse and stalked me."

"I don't know what John wanted, and I don't care! If you must know he divorced me, but he was the one chasing around. Why he is calling and texting me repeatedly, I have no idea."

"Oh dear," Cathy muttered. "Could it have something to do with your kids?"

"No, I called them, and they are fine. I didn't tell them their father is here in London pestering me."

"Perhaps you ought to find out what he wants," Cathy suggested.

"And where exactly is this Colin?" Victoria asked.

Charlotte took a deep breath and gulped back some wine. "Colin is the love of my life. He is a marine biologist and went missing three years ago." She quickly explained how she'd called the police and how she'd tried to trace him but without success.

Lou became melancholy. "It's terrible to have to wait and wait for someone who never shows up," she muttered. "I am so sorry, Charlotte."

The women exchanged glances, obviously surprised by Lou's

empathy.

Victoria took charge. "There must be a way to find out what happened to Colin. We could check marine records or something."

"I've tried all that, including contacting his office to find out what ship he was on, but no one seemed to know what happened. The boat docked, he got off, and no one has seen him since."

"He might have been kidnapped. We can offer a reward for information," Lizzie, who had no money, offered.

"What about the American Embassy? Wouldn't they help?"

"He's British," Charlotte said just as her phone vibrated. "For goodness's sake! It's John again."

"Answer it," Victoria, she who must be obeyed, commanded. "Maybe he knows something."

"I doubt that. He never even met Colin." Reluctantly, Charlotte clicked on the phone. "Yes, John, what do you want?"

John's voice on the phone was barely audible. Charlotte's face turned white. "I am so sorry, John. You can certainly stay at my house to recover. Come on over later tonight. I'll get the guest room ready."

After she discontinued the conversation, she told the wide-eyed and intrigued ladies that John had colon cancer and was here in London at a Cleveland Clinic where one of the top surgeons, an American doctor known to be best in the field, had started him on treatments and was planning surgery in a few days.

Cathy looked stricken. "That poor man!" she cried.

All eyes turned on her. "Have you gotten your biopsy results yet?" Victoria asked quietly.

Cathy put her beer stein on the coffee table. "Just a second," she said, heading for the kitchen. She came back with an official-looking envelope and waved it in the air. "It's from St. Thomas's. I could not bear to open it."

"Give it here!" Victoria snatched it from her and tore it open. She spent a few moments perusing the contents. "Good news!" she announced. "No cancer! They want you to follow up with your doctor though."

Cathy began to cry, and they all gathered around her and wrapped their arms around one another.

Chapter Eight

Lizzie

Lizzie felt tears well up in her eyes as they each comforted a relieved Cathy. While she was still smarting a little at Victoria's abrupt insistence that she open the letter, she was glad   poor Cathy no longer had to worry.

In fact, she pondered, it wasn't just that that had pissed her off about Victoria. It was the way she had demanded Charlotte explain her missing husband, and how she was so rude to Lou. Okay, Lou was a tough cookie, and that kind of thing was water off a duck's back to her, but still…

Lizzie sighed. If she was honest, there were a lot of things about Victoria that were beginning to annoy her lately, and she'd found herself, more and more, contemplating their relationship.

It had begun as a friendship and, whilst it wasn't sexual, the friendship had deepened to love, but on reflection Lizzie wondered if it was love. Or was it her need to be looked after, to be wanted?

Victoria was so dominant in their relationship, often speaking for her, doing things she thought were helpful, but which Lizzie now started to realise, felt controlling. She was stifled, smothered by Victoria and she knew she'd have to do something about it.

"To good health!" Lou suddenly cheered, holding up her wine glass, and Cathy smiled, her happy tears still wet on her face. "To good health and the Second Chance Saloon!" she cheered back, at which Lou smiled smugly, but Lizzie didn't miss the loud tsk from the disapproving Victoria by her side.

"So, tell us more about the show." Lizzie asked Lou, feeling Victoria flinch next to her. She knew she'd be fuming that Lizzie had given Lou a platform to show off, and wondered if that was why she'd done it.

"I am the HOST!" Lou beamed and launched into an excited babble about her new project.

Lizzie took a moment to glance at Victoria who at that moment was pretending to stifle a fake yawn. Her heckles rose. "Just what is your problem, Victoria?" The words had left her mouth before she could even process them and the silence that ensued was deafening.

"Excuse me!" Victoria was open-mouthed, the shock visible on her face, and Lizzie felt her heart speed up, but she'd started now.

"Why do you have to be so rude to Lou?" Lizzie was on a roll now, her frustration at Victoria boiling over.

"Rude to me, Doll? Is she?" Lou exclaimed and Lizzie almost laughed.

"I don't, erm, what do you...?" For once, Victoria was lost for words and Lizzie suddenly felt sorry for her, regretting her impetuous remarks.

"Oh, forget it," Lizzie waved her hand at Victoria, hoping to wash it all away but Victoria had found her voice again.

"Oh no you don't. What is *your* problem? How dare you jump down my throat like that, just who do you...?"

Cathy stood up quickly. "Ladies, please, let's not fall out..."

"I disagree," Lou chimed in, "this is pure drama!"

Charlotte cleared her throat, "Cathy's right, let's all calm down."

Victoria eyed Lizzie squarely, one eyebrow raised in challenge, and Lizzie knew she'd gone too far.

"Sorry," she muttered, her gaze turned to the floor.

"Yes, me too. Sorry I came tonight." Victoria picked up her bag from the floor. "Cathy, thanks for hosting, glad you're in the clear with your health. Unfortunately, I'm not staying here a moment longer." With that, she turned on her heel and left the room. The banging of the front door made the other four ladies flinch and Lizzie sighed.

"Sorry," she repeated. "I don't know what's gotten into me tonight."

Cathy stroked her arm comfortingly. "It's been pretty emotional. Maybe we should call it a day."

"Yes," Charlotte agreed, eagerly standing up.

"What, wait! What about my show? I haven't finished telling you about my show!" Lou pouted, her shiny, bright red lips suddenly looking huge. *Has she had fillers?* Lizzie thought randomly.

"Another time, Lou." Cathy wearily ushered them to the hallway, exhaustion etched across her face.

As they said their goodbyes, with Lou marching huffily off down the street, well, marching as much as she could in those ridiculous heels, and Charlotte almost sprinting to get to the sanctuary of her home, Lizzie heard a ping from her mobile phone.

Pulling it from her bag with a sinking feeling, she saw she had a text from Victoria.

Tentatively, she pressed the message icon to read the full body.

I have just one question... She read, and frowned at her phone, perplexed.

What? She quickly typed back, fearing the worst, was Victoria going to ask her if she still loved her? Did she? Was she ready to admit it if she didn't?

Her phone pinged for a second time, and she quickly read the reply.

Are we ever going to discuss that damn book?!

Lizzie snorted back a laugh, and her shoulders sagged in relief. She was forgiven, for now.

There would be a time when their discussion needed to take place but tonight was not it. Lizzie quickly typed a laughing emoji to Victoria and began the short walk home, her mind fluttering with doubts and decisions. Tonight, she would sleep on it. Tomorrow was another day.

Chapter Nine

Charlotte

Charlotte sank onto her couch and stared out of the window at the rain splashing down onto the street. In her hand was a large bar of Cadbury's milk chocolate. She usually limited how much she ate, but this evening, after a thorough cleaning of her house in preparation for the arrival of her ex, John, she felt a serious need for comfort. Her spare bedroom was ready with clean sheets and blankets, a bedside lamp sat on the nightstand so he could read at night, and she'd even dragged up a TV from a storage closet and put it on the dresser so he'd have something to watch once he came home from the surgery. The last thing she'd done was move all the clothes out from the drawers and the built-in closet, some of them Colin's. She considered putting his photo somewhere out of sight, but that would be ridiculous. There was no way any reconciliation of her relationship with John was about to happen. She was merely being a good person, helping the father of her children in his time of need.

Speaking of children, she picked up the phone. They must not know about their dad. Clearly, when she'd talked to them earlier, they'd had no idea what he was doing in England. Equally clearly, he didn't want to tell them, typical of him to hide important matters, especially if they made him look weak. She was better off without him and had known that for years. Dear Colin, she gazed at his photo and let the tears flow. What had happened to him? He was no philanderer, and she completely trusted him. Theirs had been a sweet coupling, not only in bed but in their consideration of one another and encouragement of each other. He'd helped her get her teaching job in England, and she'd encouraged his overseas explorations.

She plopped the last piece of chocolate into her mouth and hardly tasted it, trying to remember if John looked sick when he'd barged in on the book club meeting. Was he already on chemo? Had he lost hair? Was he nauseous? Maybe she ought to provide a bedpan and a bucket in case. Dear God, this was an agony, and the chocolate had not helped but if she'd had another bar, she would have stuffed it in her mouth.

Well John, she thought, dialling her son's number back in the states. *Well John, I don't answer to you, and the kids have a right to know what's going on. What if you die? They'll never forgive me for not telling them.*

When her son picked up, she almost panicked but of course he knew it was her and she couldn't just hang up. "Hello, Mom," he answered, sounding sleepy. And she realis   ed it was six in the morning at his house. "Hi J.J.," she said. "I hope I didn't wake you."

"Not really. I was just having a quick cup of coffee before my morning jog. What's up?"

She quickly filled him in about his father.

"I knew there was something going on," JJ said. "Especially when he didn't answer any of my calls. It's good of you to let him stay with you. Tell you what, I have some vacation due. I'll come over to help you take care of him."

"There's no need, JJ," Charlotte cried. "I'll manage."

JJ, shortened from John Junior, was so much like his father: stubborn and pushy. He could not be dissuaded, so she reluctantly told him to book a flight and let her know when he'd be coming into Heathrow, which wasn't too far from her house so she could easily pick him up. "Dear God," she cried, seeing a cab pull up in front of her house. "Here's your dad now. I have to go. Let your sister know what's happening. I'll call her as soon as I can." She rushed out the door to the curb and took his wheelie from the cabdriver who'd plucked it from the boot. John paid the driver and waited uneasily, obviously at a loss for words. "Hi, Charlotte," he managed.

"Is this all the luggage you've got?" Charlotte asked, remembering he always travelled light, no doubt trying to hide from her what he was up to. But that was water over the dam, and she intended to be kind. But it wasn't going to be easy as old feelings of resentment surged. "I have a room ready for you," she announced. "Follow me."

As the days passed, they fell into a quiet routine. He was still undergoing some pre-surgery treatments and always took a minicab to and from the hospital. He stayed in his room most of the time and there was little other than polite conversation with him. Until she told him she was going to the airport to pick up their son, JJ.

"I didn't want them to know," he shouted, reminding her of the rows they'd had after he'd announced he was divorcing her, as if it had been her fault.

"Too bad!" she answered mildly. "Your children have a right to know, and I am not going to be the one to tell lies to anyone. Try to be happy that JJ loves you enough to even come." With that, she soon pulled her car out of the garage and set off for the airport. It would actually be a relief to have JJ in the house and hopefully it would break the tension that was like smog, making it hard to breathe. Even the cat was on edge and off her food.

She quickly made it to the waiting area outside of customs. The flight was in and soon people started pouring through the lines and emerging from the security desks to pick up their luggage. Her heart fluttered at the prospect of seeing her son but when she saw his head and shoulders taller than the person behind him, she exclaimed out loud, "Oh my God!" causing people to turn around looking concerned.

Behind JJ came her daughter, tired and travel-weary, but as pretty as ever. As soon as they could, they hugged. "I wasn't expecting you, Sue!" she murmured into her daughter's hair.

"I know, Mommy, but I figured you might need more support."

"How's Dad?" JJ asked.

Charlotte resisted saying he was a pain in the you know what, because actually he wasn't, it was just awkward. "He'll be glad you've come."

Meanwhile her mind was racing with how in the world she was going to accommodate both her son and her daughter. It wasn't as if she could put them in the same bed as she'd once had to do when they were little. There was the couch of course.

On the way home, her phone announced a call from, of all people, Lou. She let it go to voicemail, planning to call her back later.

Once she'd gotten the kids into the house and left them with their father who was making a cup of tea, her cell chimed. Lou again. "I have to take this!" she told them and went up to her bedroom. *What?* She thought to herself. *Did John think he could be English and settle everyone down with hot tea? A hot toddy or a strong shot of Scotch was usually more to his liking.*

"What do you want, Lou?" she said curtly, knowing she sounded frazzled and angry.

"Hey, babe, I wanted to make sure you put the date down for your week in Hertfordshire in a fabulous country house for the first, the very first episode of Second Chance Saloon. By then you'll probably need the break from what's his name, your ex, Jimmy."

"No. It's John. My daughter has shown up unexpectedly and I've nowhere comfortable for her to sleep. John has got the spare room, and I've put JJ in my office. Where on earth am I supposed to put Sue. The couch is too short."

"No worries," Lou said. "Sue can stay in my spare bedroom. I've got two and I'll be gone most of the time anyway on the set getting everything prepared."

Charlotte's jaw fell open in shock. Lou must have gone mad being so accommodating, but maybe she'd misjudged her. Could she inflict Lou upon her daughter? Then again, who knows, they both were theatre lovers, maybe they'd get along? And her flat wasn't far away. And Lou owed her for having almost destroyed her white rug. "I'll have to let you know, Lou," she muttered.

Chapter Ten

Victoria

Victoria felt antsy. She hadn't spoken to Lizzie in days and, after her outburst the other week, she was beginning to wonder if Lizzie was having doubts about their relationship.

Victoria knew she could come across as a little controlling, but it came from a good place. She wanted things to be just so, everything to run smoothly as clockwork. Maybe Lizzie was feeling stifled after suffering so much abuse at the hands of her ex-husband, and misjudged Victoria's manner as similar to his.

She knew Lizzie had been through a lot with her ex, Chris. He was a giant of a man that, Victoria was sure, Lizzie must have been hugely attracted to when they met. But for years, he had manipulated and controlled Lizzie to a point where she didn't know who she was anymore. That's why Victoria thought she could help her, to guide her, to look after her. Lizzie had loved it at first, she thought. Loved her. When Chris finally left her, Victoria couldn't do enough for Lizzie. She was there whilst she cried, desperately questioning what she had done wrong. She had held her, reassured her and eventually fallen in love with her.

Though there wasn't a sexual side to their relationship, Victoria had experienced moments when she had felt something more might happen. Lizzie though, had, right from the start made it clear that her intentions were strictly nonsexual, and Victoria accepted that.

For Victoria, just being with Lizzie was enough. Just to hold her hand and sit in silence was plenty for her, but maybe she had pushed things a little too hard. After all, maybe Lizzie needed more time, more space; it wasn't even a year since Chris left.

Victoria knew she could be headstrong, pushing full steam ahead when others are happy to merely plod along. Not her, she had no time for plodding. *Maybe that's what drove Tom away,* she wondered.

Tom had been (she thought) the love of her life many, many, years ago. The one that got away, she mentally referred to him. He'd told her she was breaking him, that he feared he was losing himself. She hadn't understood, at first. She thought he liked the fact she wanted to hear every last detail about how his day had been, who he had spoken to. But no, for Tom, it was too much. Little did he know the dark secret that burdened Victoria, the secret she could never tell that explained her fear of being abandoned. The secret which fuelled her insecurities.

Tom's final words to her as he departed her life: "You're a jealous, controlling harridan, and I've had enough, Victoria. I've had enough."

Was that the same with Lizzie? Had *she* had enough?

She needed to talk to Lizzie, to explain.

She picked up her mobile phone, intending to send a jokey text message, just to break the silence between them, but quickly thought better of it. She threw her phone on the sofa and sat down next to it.

Why was she suddenly feeling so insecure again? This just wasn't like her; she was always in control of everything: life, emotions, Lizzie?

Sighing, she watched her cat, Biscuit, on the armchair across the room, beginning to groom himself. *More fur for me to scrape up,* she mused. She picked up her phone again, scrolling through her last messages with Lizzie, trying to see if there were any signs of her waning interest. Maybe Victoria was just reading too much into Lizzie's outburst.

"That's it!" She stood suddenly, causing a startled Biscuit to dart from the armchair and out the lounge door. "I'll go and speak to Lizzie. Face to face, heart to heart." With an assertive nod, she climbed the stairs to change. She wanted, no, needed to look her best. She'd clear the air with Lizzie and all would be fine.

Just as she reached the top stair, she heard the ping of her mobile phone back in the living room. *Lizzie? Please please, let it be Lizzie.* She galloped back down the stairs, two at a time, and grabbed for her phone.

"Yes!" She punched the air; it was a message from Lizzie.

With a triumphant grin on her face, she opened the text.

"We need to talk," was the ominous message.

Chapter Eleven

Lou

Lou sank into a cushiony red chair and rested a glass ashtray full of cigarette butts on one of the rolled arms. She kicked off her high heels and sank her feet into a black shag rug. "Make yourself at home, Doll," she said to Charlotte's daughter, Sue. "Smoke?" she offered the girl one of her Silk Cuts, waving the white packet in the air.

Sue declined, taking a seat on a fancy yellow sofa opposite a fake fireplace. Lou's lounge was an assortment of modern furniture, none of it matching, and all pricey, except for a scratched side table that looked about a hundred years old.

Seeing Sue eying it curiously, Lou took a long drag on her cigarette and blew smoke in the air. "That is the only thing left of my mother's. She wanted little tables where she could put her teacup, but my father said they couldn't afford such luxuries." Lou rolled her eyes. "I bought that one for her with earnings from the first TV ad I made for women's underwear."

"How kind."

"It made her happy. And isn't that what life is for, to be happy? Speaking of which, how about some wine? Glasses are in the cabinet above the sink. You're tall like me and should easily reach them. Bring the long-stemmed ones, okay?"

Lou watched Sue obediently head into the kitchen. It seemed odd to have someone in her flat but at least there would be someone here for Peregrine, and even if the cat ignored the girl, she could still clean the cat litter on a regular basis.

Sue came back in with two long stemmed wine glasses and a bottle of Pinot Grigio. She sat them on the small table that belonged to Lou's mother. "Shall I pour?"

"Please!" Lou answered, enjoying the attention. "Do you like cats?"

"I love all animals, but when I went into the kitchen, your cat jumped down from the counter and fled. What an unusual cat! What's her name?"

"Peregrine. *He's* a Manx. He'll warm up to you once you start giving him his Chocka Chicken I have delivered. His cat litter is in the kitchen, and he likes it cleaned often." Lou raised a questioning eyebrow at Sue.

"Sure, I'll take care of him when you're gone. I appreciate getting to stay with you."

"Sure thing!" Lou imitated an American accent in an exaggerated drawl.

"It must be exciting to be an actress."

"Sure is!" Lou replied, knowing full well her life had been filled with difficulty, hardly making enough money to pay her bills. But that was about to change with Second Chance Saloon. "Say," she continued in her American accent, "fetch some cheese and crackers, okay?"

"I'll be happy to get them for you, but my brother and I are taking Dad out to dinner, so I don't want to spoil my appetite."

"Doll," Lou grinned, "drink up! You are in for a treat! I'm going to give you a makeover."

Lou could see Sue had possibilities that some mascara, eyeshadow, heavy foundation to cover her blotchy skin, gleaming rouge, glossy lipstick and maybe some sparkles would enhance.

"There's no need," Sue said. "I'm not much for makeup."

"You want to be beautiful for your dinner, don't you? Bring your wine. Come along." Lou grabbed Sue's arm and led her into her bedroom and sat her down in front of a white makeup vanity and turned on the lights around the mirror. Sue sighed as Lou spun her around to face her and began fussing over her. "Much better," Lou remarked, sipping her wine, and spinning Sue around to see herself in the mirror. The girl's eyes, emphasized by sparkly green eyeshadow and long black eyelashes, looked startled. She glanced at her watch. "I need to go!"

"I'll walk with you to your mum's."

Charlotte opened the door for them. "Sue," she cried. "You look like a tart!"

"Oh please!" Lou grinned. "She's ready for a night out on the town."

"With her father!" came a deep male voice from the lounge. Charlotte's ex stepped into the entranceway and hugged his daughter. But his eyes rested on Lou's cleavage. "You must be the actress." He let go of Sue and reached out his hand which Lou happily took. She felt a spark of attraction and was pleased when he held onto her hand longer than necessary.

Chapter Twelve

Charlotte

Charlotte was relieved when John, Sue and JJ finally left for their dinner, but peeved that Lou was still there, hovering in the entranceway.

"Lou, thank you for taking Sue in, I'm really grateful, but I'm so tired, I was going to get an early night."

Lou waved her comment away and strode into the living room. "You'll sleep enough when you're dead, Doll! Come on, let's have some vino and a catch up."

With a sinking heart, Charlotte went into the kitchen for the wine and glasses. There was no point in resisting. Lou was not going anywhere. She sighed and wandered back to the living room.

"So, when are you next off to Hertfordshire?" she enquired politely.

"Well," Lou was suddenly animated, even more so than her usual full-on exuberance, "that's what I wanted to talk to you about."

"Oh?" Charlotte raised an eyebrow, despair settling into her belly.

"Yes, I spoke to my producer. He's agreed that I can choose the female contestants, so it's game on! And you, my dear, are first up!"

"Oh goodness," Charlotte stood up, her hand to her mouth as she shook her head furiously. "No, no," she repeated. "I know you mentioned it, Lou, but it didn't register at the time. I couldn't possibly be on the show, not now with everything that's going on with John."

Lou stood beside her, taking her arm, a bright smile on her heavily made-up face. "Of course, you can, Doll!"

"No way!" Charlotte backed away from Lou, knowing that for the first time in her life she needed to assert herself. "Absolutely not, Lou, No way!"

"But it's all been arranged…" Lou pleaded like a petulant child.

36

"Then you'll just have to un-arrange it. I mean it, Lou, this is not happening."

Charlotte felt suddenly exhausted. This assertiveness thing, whilst it was all well and good, was tiring work.

"Please, Charlotte!"

Charlotte was stunned to see tears in Lou's eyes. Was she really so unused to not getting her own way that it made her cry?

"No, Lou. And that's final." Charlotte gave herself a mental pat on the back, pleased with how she was standing her ground.

"But I'm going to look like a complete idiot if I tell my producer now!" Lou's eyes had dried, her sadness now turned to a rage that uglified her face.

"I don't care. You shouldn't have said anything without speaking to me first." Charlotte was quite literally dead on her feet, desperate for Lou to leave.

"I did speak to you!" Lou retorted.

"When I was distracted with the John thing!" Charlotte flung back. "If I'd even registered what you had said, there's no way I would have agreed to it. I thought it was just more of your…" Charlotte paused, knowing she'd gone too far.

"More of my what, Charlotte?" Lou raised her dramatic eyebrows, as much as the Botox-filled forehead would allow, anyway, and waited for Charlotte to respond.

"It doesn't matter," Charlotte muttered.

"Oh, I think it does. More of my what, Charlotte? My drama, my what?"

Lou wanted an answer, that was for sure, and Charlotte wanted her gone, so with a deep breath and another mental pat on the back, she looked directly into Lou's eyes.

"More of your lies, okay. I thought it was more of your lies."

As if her final words had taken the last of her strength, Charlotte sank back into the sofa, unable to look at Lou any longer,

She heard the outraged gasp though and waited for the torrent of abuse to come her way, but when she spoke, Lou's voice was eerily calm.

"Well, thank you very much, Charlotte. You'll regret this, you mark my words."

Lou picked up her glass and drained the wine before gently placing it on the coffee table and leaving the room. The shutting, not slamming, of the front door, left a ghostly chill in the air.

"What the hell just happened?" Charlotte spoke aloud into the empty room. "And where the hell will Sue stay now?"

Chapter Thirteen

Victoria

Outside the White Bear Pub, Victoria smelled beer and chips, neither of which she much liked. She hesitated before pushing the door open to go in. She could hear people talking and laughing and glasses chinking. She only hoped she would end up laughing too but she dreaded what Lizzie was going to say, and it was not like her to fret about what anyone thought. After being in the daylight, it seemed dark inside with only a few lit candles on tables, and a subtle overhead chandelier. This pub was posher than most and served quite a variety of dinner stuff, but she knew Lizzie loved fish and chips, and she stopped by the bar and ordered two dinners along with two glasses of red wine.

After putting in her order, she narrowed her eyes and surveyed the tables looking for Lizzie but didn't see her. "I'll be over there," she told the barman and pointed to a booth on a far wall beyond the bar. She sidestepped people at tall round bar tables and made her way to the booth, sliding into the seat so she could see the door. She opened her phone. She was five minutes late and usually Lizzie was on time.

While she waited, she heard American voices at a nearby booth and turned to look. A man with dark hair had his back to her, and opposite were a couple of kids in their twenties. They reminded her of Charlotte's children who she'd seen in photos on the mantelpiece, except the girl was smothered in makeup. The wine and fish and chips were delivered just as Lizzie came into the pub. "Yoo hoo!" Victoria stood up and waved.

Upon seeing her, Lizzie hurried over. "I'm sorry I'm late. I was on the phone with Lou." As she sat down, she stared at the plate of fish and chips. "What's this?"

"I thought you'd enjoy them," Victoria said. "And here's a glass of

Cabernet Sauvignon for you." As soon as Lizzie had shrugged off her jacket, Victoria set the glass of red wine in front of her. "This is your favourite, right?"

Lizzie sighed. "That's just it, Victoria. I can order my own dinner. That's what I wanted to talk to you about."

"Dinners?" Victoria said, jokingly, trying to lighten the moment.

"Of course not. I wanted to say sorry for being so rude to you the other day, and I want you to know how much I truly appreciate your friendship, but I need to make my own decisions and regain my confidence."

"I get it," Victoria said. "I'll try not to be so bossy. I'll send the dinner back and you can get whatever you like. I'll pay."

"Stop it! Stop telling me what to do!"

Victoria, scared of what else Lizzie might say, leaned across the table, trying to change the subject, and gestured at the nearby booth. "They sound like Yanks. Do you think they're Charlotte's kids, and that guy, from behind, looks like her ex. The girl looks as tarty as Lou!"

"It probably is them. Sue, Charlotte's daughter, is staying in Lou's spare bedroom while her father gets his surgery and recovers at Charlotte's. She didn't have enough room for both her kids along with her ex. Lou told me she helped Sue with her makeup."

"I would have been glad to put Sue up to save her from that witch!" Victoria had a sinking feeling that Lizzie was replacing her with, of all people, Lou. It was an unbearable thought. "What on earth were you doing chatting with Lou anyway?" Her voice was loud enough to get the attention of Charlotte's ex, who glanced over his shoulder.

"Lou called to invite me to the Second Chance Saloon. The thing is, Victoria, I want a second chance. I want to enjoy a holiday in Hertfordshire, and if there's another man for me, I am going to go for it!"

"But Lizzie," Victoria began, not sure of how to proceed. "Are you forgetting how Chris abused you and belittled you and stalked you?"

"All men aren't like Chris. I might even ask Lou to fix my makeup and hair. I could use some sexy clothes too."

"You must have lost your mind!" Victoria retorted and felt like getting up and storming out but suddenly realised she always ran away when she was angry rather than stay and try to talk things out. "I'm sorry, Lizzie," she managed. "I find you beautiful just as you are." She gazed at Lizzie who looked away.

Just then the Yank got up and shuffled over to their table. "You're Charlotte's friends." He grinned at Victoria. "I'm sorry I scared you," he muttered. "I am really quite harmless."

"Nothing scares me!" Victoria stared hostilely up at him, but she *was* scared to see Lizzie looking at her strangely.

Lizzie gently laid her hand on Victoria's and smiled thoughtfully. "It's okay. Not all men are evil." She glanced up at John with a wry smile before looking back at Victoria. "Maybe we *all* deserve a second chance with a good man."

Victoria felt as if a lightning bolt had hit her and opened up her mind. She took her hand back and took a long sip of wine. She was not about to reveal her sudden, or perhaps not so sudden, insight. Even as a young girl she'd known she liked other girls in forbidden ways. She'd married the guy she insisted was the love of her life because she wanted him to cure her and make her feel respectable. Their sex had always been, for her, an act of hope, but she'd never felt turned on by him, no matter how hard he tried to please her. She'd had a sharp tongue with him. He'd let her down. But in reality, she'd not been true to herself.

As Charlotte's ex excused himself, looking slightly embarrassed, she turned her eyes on Lizzie. She'd pretended to be happy with their platonic friendship, but that was all fake for Victoria. She wanted cuddles in bed, and the truth was, she wanted those cuddles to be with other women. She'd known all along that Lizzie did not share those feelings, but she'd hoped if she was nice enough and giving enough, that could change. "Oh dear," she moaned, realising that her sharp controlling manner with Tom was all a cover up for her shame at herself. But as fearless as she presented herself, she had no idea if she'd ever have the courage to come out and admit she was a lesbian and always had been.

Chapter Fourteen

Lou

"Rolling in five minutes, Lou!" Mike, the floor manager, called over his shoulder as he strode past Lou in the make-up room.

"You got it!" She trilled after him, gazing at herself in the mirror. "A little more blusher, don't you think?" Lou asked Trixie, who was currently dabbing a powder brush over Lou's nose.

"I really think you have enough, what with the lights and everything, you don't want overkill." Trixie held her breath, waiting for the diva-like response she would usually get from the major players on a production set.

"Sure, Doll, whatever you think. You're the expert!" Lou beamed at Trixie, who hurriedly slicked off the red lip gloss that had bled onto Lou's chin.

"Three minutes, Lou!" One of the runners, a young intern with bright red hair and a dreadful case of acne, whizzed towards her. "Where's Lizzie?"

"Lizzie is…" Lou looked around the make-up room, "well, she *was* just here." She turned to Trixie, "did you see where she went?"

Trixie shrugged, "Morag did her hair and makeup, so I don't know."

"Well can someone find out?" Lou's voice was suddenly shrill. The last thing she needed was Lizzie going missing, just as they were about to shoot the first episode. It was embarrassing enough when she'd had to explain to her producer about Charlotte's no-show. If Lizzie has gotten cold feet, this would be a disaster.

Lou quickly grabbed her mobile phone and pressed Lizzie's contact details.

"Lou?"

With a gasp of relief that Lizzie had picked up, Lou relaxed. "Where are you, Doll?"

"I'm erm, I'm just in the loo, I erm…"

Lou's heart sank as she heard the uncertainty in Lizzie's voice. "You're not backing out on me, are you?" Lou held her breath as she waited for Lizzie's response. "Elizabeth!" Lou was stern: this was not going to happen.

"No, no, I'm not backing out. I'm on my way. See you in a second."

Lou breathed easy again as Lizzie hung up, then plastered a smile on her caked-up face. She stood and turned to the minions around her. "Showtime!" Strutting on her stiletto heels, holding up the black satin of her floor-length dress, so as not to step on it, Lou walked onto the studio floor; a makeshift area set in the grounds of the Hertfordshire house.

Spotting Lizzie, her heart sank. *What was she wearing?* Sure, contestants were allowed to choose their own outfits, but Lizzie hadn't even made an effort. Her three-quarter-length beige cropped trousers, teamed with a mud-brown button shirt, and the most hideous Birkenstock sandals did nothing for her. *Oh Lizzie.* Lou shook her head in despair, silently cursing, again, Charlotte's decision to pull out. At least Charlotte had some style, albeit not on the same par as she, Lou. But Lizzie?

"Hey Lou," Lizzie approached her, a nervous smile on her plain face. *Jeez, she didn't even have much makeup on!*

"Lizzie, dear, are you not going to get changed?" Lou knew she was being a bitch, but she was furious at Lizzie's lack of effort.

Lizzie looked down at herself self-consciously. "I, erm, I am changed. I thought, well the producer said to be ourselves. You know, show our true personality in order to find the right match."

Lou bit her tongue, just short of stopping herself from retorting that was fine if her perfect match was Mr. Bean! "Well, yes, but…"

"Let's go ladies!" Mike the floor manager interrupted them, clapping his hands and gesturing for Lou to take her place on the sofa, where she would open the show and then bring on the first contestant: Lizzie.

Ah well, nothing I can do now. Lizzie's probably only doing it to put some steam into stuck up Victoria anyway! Lou chuckled to herself as she made her way to the seating area and took her place, her smile fixed and her heart racing as she heard the opening title music.

Chapter Fifteen

Cathy

Cathy hesitated at the front door, almost hoping Charlotte wouldn't be home. But she heard light footsteps approaching and it was too late to back out.

"Cathy!" Charlotte exclaimed. "How nice to see you. Come on in."

Cathy followed her into the living room, noticing a pile of men's clothes on one of the chairs. She knew Charlotte's son was staying here and also her ex-husband. She bet Charlotte disliked the disruption to her everything-in-its-place-life. Charlotte's kindness to her ex, a man she didn't much like, gave Cathy hope. When she'd tried to explain to Lou why she couldn't come to the second episode of Second Chance Saloon, the hostess had been furious. "You tell Charlotte to come instead, then," she yelled.

So here she was at Charlotte's, with no idea how to persuade her to be on television. "Did you watch Lizzie on the show?" she asked, putting off the real reason for her visit.

"I did. Lou ought to have helped her with her wardrobe. The poor thing looked like she'd been dragged through a hedge backwards."

"I felt sorry for her too and asked Lou to help me choose appropriate clothing to wear. I'm supposed to be on next. Lou is taking me to Harrod's and said the show will cover any costs. It's a great opportunity, but..."

"But what?" Charlotte smiled. "I daresay you don't want to end up being tarted up like Lou."

"Lou is Lou," Cathy said diplomatically.

"One of a kind!" Charlotte responded. "I have time for a cup of tea if you'd like one, but then I have to head to the hospital to see how John is doing with the preoperative testing. My son and daughter are with him, and I want to give them a break."

"You are always so nice, Charlotte. I would love a cup of tea, but only if you've got time. Or coffee would be great." She knew her American friend probably preferred coffee.

"Sure. Come on in the kitchen with me while I put on the coffee pot. I even have cream if you want some. That's what my son and ex prefer. Me, I like it straight."

"I'll pass on the cream. Diet, you know."

"So, when are they taping the next show? It's not live, is it?"

"It is live. I'm due on set in a few days, but I have a little problem that I'm hoping you can help me with."

"I'll try," Charlotte said quizzically.

"I saw my doctor, and he wants me to have my ovary removed because of the cyst. The sooner the better. And as it happens the surgeon has an opening tomorrow. It's supposed to be a simple laser thing and I'll be out in one day, but you never know if there will be complications."

"Poor you," Charlotte moaned.

"I was hoping you'd go on the show in my place. I simply cannot put off this surgery or the cyst might become cancerous." Cathy knew she was exaggerating, but she really did hate to let Lou down. She was disappointed she wouldn't get to wear something pretty, had even thought how wonderful it would be to wear a long gown, something that would hide her bulges and make her feel beautiful.

"You do know I told Lou that in no way would I appear on her show?"

"But why not?" Cathy asked.

"I've just got too much on my plate right now, and I don't want any more stress, and besides, I need to prepare lessons for the next term."

Cathy sensed there was more to Charlotte's adamant refusal to be on TV than her worry about stress or lesson preparation. She knew too how embarrassed Charlotte was about her marital situation, but she suddenly had an idea. A good idea! "What if your husband, Colin, has amnesia and that's why he's been missing? If you go on the air, maybe he'll see you and his memory might be jogged."

"It's highly unlikely!" Charlotte retorted, pouring them each a mug of coffee.

"Probably, but you never know," Cathy said optimistically, well aware that amnesia was usually temporary. She took her mug and followed Charlotte into the lounge. "Colin looks like a great guy," she remarked looking at the photo on the mantel. "It must be awful for you not knowing where he is or what happened to him."

"I miss him," Charlotte remarked, "and I certainly don't want another man in my life."

"Of course not," Cathy said. "I wonder what men Lou is going to drag onto her show. Poor Lizzie, the way she looked, is likely to be paired up with a hobo. I wish we could help her. I'm not much better dressed than her, though."

"Don't put yourself down, Cath. You've got plenty to offer and looks aren't everything. In fact, at our age, companionship and civility are far more important."

"I know. But I did hope Lou would help find me a partner. She's furious with me now and probably won't let me on the show ever."

Charlotte sipped her drink thoughtfully. "Let me know the exact details of your expected appearance, and if I can, I will step in for you. I plan on being at the hospital with my kids when John gets his operation, so I can't guarantee I'd be available."

Cathy set her cup down, went over to Charlotte and wrapped her arms around her. "Thank you so much!"

Chapter Sixteen

Victoria

Victoria had watched Lizzie on Lou's first show, and her heart had sunk seeing her friend obviously nervous, dressed in her usual shabby clothing. Why on earth hadn't she got something smarter to wear? Hadn't she mentioned only the other day that she wanted Lou to give her a makeover? As she made herself a cup of tea, the phone rang. She almost ignored it but at the last moment, even though it wasn't a familiar number, she answered. "Hello," she said.

"Victoria, thank God!" she heard Lou's voice.

"What is it?" she cried, worried something had happened to Lizzie.

"It's Lizzie." Lou moaned dramatically. "I don't know what to do with her."

Victoria sank onto a kitchen chair. "What are you talking about, Lou?"

"You have to come and fetch her," she answered.

"Oh my God! Is she okay?

"No, she's not." Lou gave an exaggerated sigh. "You'd think she just lost out on an Oscar, the way she's carrying on."

"What on earth do you mean?" Victoria wished she could slap some sense into Lou.

"Well, she won't stop crying and she's sweating profusely."

"Call a doctor or take her to the emergency room!" Victoria said, remembering a friend with diabetes who'd gone into hypoglycaemic shock. That friend had died. "Now, Lou!" she shouted.

"One of the crew took her blood pressure. It's high, but he thinks she's having a panic attack. You've got to come to calm her down."

"Dear God, how am I supposed to get to Hertfordshire. I don't have a car."

Victoria heard Lou telling Lizzie that she, Victoria, was on her way. Then Lou said into the phone, "Just hearing you are coming seems to have helped. She stopped sobbing. Please come. And hurry."

~ * ~

On the way home in the cab that Victoria would rather not pay for despite her inheritance, Lizzie, who was pale and overwrought, hung her head. "I publicly made a fool of myself," she lamented. "I am so embarrassed. The producer or director told me to be myself and that they wanted me to look messy, but Lou was furious and insisted that in any future episode I'd have to do better. But more than that, I called my ex an arsehole loser."

"He *was* a creep!" Victoria said. "You only spoke the truth."

"But, Victoria, I *swore* publicly."

Victoria sighed deeply. "It's okay, Lizzie, nobody died!"

~ * ~

A few days later, Victoria almost felt sorry for Lou when, first, Cathy couldn't make it to the second episode where a new male contender would be introduced to the audience, and then Charlotte who was supposed to fill in for Cathy, came down with the flu and had to back out too. Lou was frantic! Victoria definitely did not want to be a part of Second Chance Saloon. It was so not her, unless she came out as gay. And wouldn't that put a crimp in Lou's style? It might even sink her show! Victoria felt no love for Lou, but wasn't mean-spirited enough to cause trouble to anyone, except abusive bastards, two-timing control freaks and narrow-minded know-it-alls. Lou was neither.

When Lou didn't call her to set up a time for her to appear on the show, she was irritated, even though Lizzie told her that Lou didn't have much say in the design of the show. There were originally meant to be the four women from the book club, one a week followed by four weeks of potential male partners. But, as it turned out, viewers had loved Lizzie in the first episode; loving her openness and vulnerability. The feedback was so positive that the network wanted her back, fast, to boost the ratings. Lizzie was a nervous wreck, and Victoria considered insisting she step in for Lizzie to save her from further nervous embarrassment. She once again mused how satisfying it would be to knock Lou off her high horse by stating on the live show that she wanted a lady partner not some needy guy the network provided.

Chapter Seventeen

Lizzie

"I'm Lizzie, I'm fifty-three, from Ickenham in Middlesex, and I'm looking for companionship."

"Well, Lizzie, after your, erm, moment in the first episode, now is your time to actually enter the Second Chance Saloon where the man of your dreams, matched according to world-beating data research, is waiting for you. Enjoy!"

Lou, standing in the entranceway, held her arms wide, gesturing for Lizzie to enter the 'Second Chance Saloon', which was actually called The Cobblers Inn, but for the duration of the show, it would enjoy its new moniker with zeal.

Lizzie took a deep breath and gulped at the cheering of the live audience on either side of the steps that were fortunately drowning out her galloping heart rate. *You can do this*, she mentally checked herself, *one foot in front of the other, that's it, come on.* She started up the stone entrance steps of the hotel, aware of the camera boom and camera guy ahead of her, thanking the Lord for her wise decision not to wear heels.

As she reached the top of the steps, the grand entrance hall just feet in front of her, a waiter, in a smart tuxedo, appeared, bearing a tray with a flute of Champagne. With a shaking hand, she took the glass, forcing herself not to gulp the whole thing down in one, and thanked the handsome young man. Lou stood aside. "Off you go," she encouraged. "Please make your way in, where your soulmate awaits you."

Another cheer came up from the outside crowd, and Lizzie walked through the doorway. The slamming of the ornate wooden doors behind her echoed in her ears as they closed.

"Wise men say..." Lizzie jumped as the music suddenly started up.

What the hell, Elvis bloody Presley? A bubble of laughter threatened to burst from her throat, but Lizzie willed herself to keep her composure.

"Lizzie?" From somewhere through a doorway, a deep voice boomed.

Lizzie stood still, startled, and suddenly a little bit fearful. Heavy footsteps approached until a large, rotund figure filled the doorframe.

"Hi, I'm Bill." The man held his hand out and Lizzie took it. "Lizzie," she replied unnecessarily.

"Shall we go through to the dining room," Bill asked, with a big smile on his face.

Bill stood to one side to allow Lizzie to step into the huge heavily beamed dining area.

"Wow," Lizzie gazed in awe at the floor to ceiling bookshelves on three of the four huge walls.

"Wonderful, isn't it?"

Lizzie finally turned back to the man, taking in his appearance for the first time.

Yes, he was portly, but tall, too. And even though her ex had been big, there was an air of kindness about this guy. His hair, whilst completely white, was at least full and the spectacles that sat on the end of his nose were far too small for his face, but they made him seem intelligent.

"Stunning," Lizzie replied, realising she hadn't yet responded to his question.

Lou's grinning voice came from the speakers. "Go on in and get to know one another and enjoy a gourmet meal."

Lizzie went ahead of Bill, trying to come up with something witty to say, but Bill had seen her response to the books. "Do you like to read?" His eyes, she noticed, were a watery pale blue, that glinted rather charmingly from behind his specs.

She chuckled softly. "It's my love of reading that got me into this crazy situation in the first place." She smiled wryly as he led the way to a huge oval dining table and pulled out a seat for her.

"How so?" He looked perplexed and she shook her head. "Just a book club thing..."

Lizzie sat down, admiring the crisp linen napkins, heavy gold-plated cutlery and crystal wine glasses that were set for two.

Bill sat opposite her, not quite as intimate as it would suggest given the vastness of the table.

"So," Bill began, "here we are."

"Yes," Lizzie scratched her neck, a habit she had when she felt awkward.

"For I can't help falling in love with you..." As Elvis reached the last crescendo, she looked at Bill, who looked at her, and together they threw their heads back and laughed raucously.

As the pair held their stomachs, their mirth making them completely uncontrollable, Lizzie felt suddenly at ease. This man had a sense of humour. Maybe, just maybe, this was going to be ok...

Meanwhile the camera cut to Lou standing on the top of the steps. "And so, we have our first couple, Bill and Lizzie, who are about to enjoy a first dinner together. Let's leave them in peace to enjoy their time together. When they are finished, we'll bring them into our studio where I'll interview them so they can learn about their hopes, dreams, and all the things we want to know about a potential mate: Is he rich? Is she religious? What kind of work do they do, and, of course, do they like sex?" The crowd applauded, and Lou smiled proudly, before the camera panned from her, clad in a leopard print jumpsuit, to Lizzie and Bill, who clinked their glasses and smiled broadly at each other, while the dulcet tones of the Bee Gee's asking them *how deep is your love,* rang around the room.

A camera followed Lou into a studio, and while periodically talking about the power of love, she explained the concept of the show a little more, in between the many commercial breaks. An hour later, Bill and Lizzie joined her and sat together on a sofa. "This is clearly love at first sight," Lou told the people watching. "Just look how solicitous Bill is of Lizzie, and she appears ten years younger, don't you think?

"Next week, I'll let you know how their relationship progresses as we wait for the arrival of our second couple. Stay tuned for episode three of Second Chance Saloon!"

Chapter Eighteen

Charlotte

Charlotte smiled as she flicked off the TV. *Bless Lizzie. It seemed she finally had herself under control! What a relief after her complete meltdown on her introduction in episode one. Now, she had finally entered the Second Chance Saloon, and she actually looked happy. Her clothes were pretty nice too, a green long-sleeved tee-shirt draped over tight blue jeans that partially hid sexy boots.*

Smiling to herself as she went into the kitchen, Charlotte pondered whether she too could do the show. After all, she had been lined up for that last episode, and, but for her convenient bout of flu, it would have been her sitting there laughing with Bill.

Charlotte sighed, was it possible for her to start afresh, find another man to be her companion? She wiped an invisible speck from the counter and flicked the kettle on, just as the door slammed shut from the hallway.

"Mom, you home?"

"In here, sweetie," she called out to her son, JJ.

"How you doing?" He pecked her on the cheek and reached for the cookie jar, reminding Charlotte of the constantly hungry teen he once was, and she smiled wistfully.

"I'm good, honey. How's your dad?"

"Yeah," JJ nodded, clearing his mouth of biscuit crumbs before he spoke, "The doctors are pleased with how the op went. Now, it's just a case of him recovering until he's well enough to come back here for his recuperation."

Charlotte nodded thoughtfully. "And did they mention how long that would likely be, his time in the hospital?"

"Oh, at least ten days if all goes well." JJ grabbed for another biscuit.

"Tea?" Charlotte asked as she pulled two mugs from the cupboard and placed a teabag in each.

Ten days, at least, till John was back here! She thought. *So, I could do the next episode!*

She picked up the now boiled kettle and poured water into each mug.

But do I really want to? Was it cheating on Colin or was there a fixed amount of time when your partner has vanished off the face of the Earth before you should move on?

And do I really want to expose myself like that? I've never been one for the spotlight. What do I even have to offer anyone?

"Earth to Mom." JJ waved his hand in front of her face. "I said no tea for me! But hey, I have some laundry for you, if you don't mind."

Without waiting for her response, JJ turned and thudded up the stairs.

"Why yes, Sir, anything you want, Sir!" Charlotte muttered under her breath and placed the lid back on the cookie jar with a roll of her eyes.

"Sod it!" She slammed her hands on the kitchen counter. "I'm going to do it. It's *my* last chance!"

And before she could dissuade herself of her decision, she grabbed up her phone and sent a short text to Lou. "I'm in."

The gentle butting on the back of her legs by Mirabelle made her smile. "Hey beautiful girl." She bent to scratch the pretty head of her furry companion, who in turn stretched her paws in front of her, a loud purr building as she was fussed.

"What do you think, my princess, can Mommy do the show?" She continued to pet the Persian who didn't have a care for what she was saying, just so long as she continued with the loving.

"Well," Charlotte whispered, "too late now." And she chuckled as she imagined Lou's face when she read her text.

Chapter Nineteen

Lou

"Peregrine," Lou called as she rushed into her flat, but the cat did not come like he usually did. Lou sighed and sank down into a chair, kicking off her high heels. Thank God Sue wasn't here. She really didn't feel like dealing with anyone else after the time she'd had with the director of her show. Any thoughts of *herself* as a star were soon dispelled to realise she had no say whatsoever about who they'd choose to put on. The casting director had insisted they bring Lizzie back, which thank God was a success or they'd likely have cancelled the show. But that big guy, Bill, who knew where they got him from? And now they were talking about bringing on another lady, rather than Charlotte, who'd only just agreed. She might be relieved, but on the other hand she'd almost certainly refuse to come on another show later. And Lou had plans for the four book club members to talk about their first kisses etc. It would be hilarious.

"Peregrine, baby," Lou called again, and when the cat did not appear, she got up and went into the kitchen. Everything was neat with dishes washed and put away, the cat litter cleaned, but no sign of the cat. "Perry, where are you!" she cried. "Stop hiding!"

Lou made her way into the bathroom hoping the cat might be in the sink, a place he liked to nap. But the only things in the sink, or rather dangling from it, were Sue's rinsed out underwear: a shabby overused bra, and cotton knickers that reminded Lou of the large navy-blue ones she'd hated to wear to gym in her school years. She had a good mind to pitch them in the garbage and provide Sue with something sexy and stylish. How did the girl ever expect a man to stay with her if he ever saw her in this dowdy and saggy lingerie? She'd never even make it to the first chance let alone the second chance.

Lou grabbed a glass of wine and sat at her kitchen table sipping. Her phone chimed and she glanced at the caller. It was, of all people, her long-time lover, Richard. Part of her wanted to jump for joy that he was calling after at least three months of ignoring her calls and texts, but another part of her wanted to ignore him. She let it go to voicemail and eventually listened to him telling her he was going to stop by her flat and wouldn't that be great? *No*, she thought, *it would not*. She needed to end this affair once and for all. She knew he was not good for her or to her. She quickly messaged him back saying she had someone staying with her, and a visit from him would be inappropriate. She didn't tell him her guest was a girl. Screw him!

Peregrine appeared out of nowhere and rubbed against her shins. "Perry, baby, at least you're here for me." She stroked the cat's back and was rewarded with a loud purr. "I hope Sue is taking good care of you." It occurred to Lou that Sue must be at the hospital now with her dad. Cathy might be in the hospital too, but with luck she'd be recovered enough to come to the show as soon as Lou needed her, if the producers allowed it.

"You know," she said to Peregrine, picking him up and cuddling him, "I have an idea of just the right person for my next episode. I'll show them all a thing or two!" She tittered to herself. Peregrine jumped down and wandered away. "I love you, baby cat, but I have to go to the hospital to make sure John and Cathy are doing okay. Well, John for sure!" She smiled to herself, put on her shoes, and called a cab.

At the reception area in the hospital Lou asked about John and Cathy. She was relieved to learn Cathy had been released to go home, and glad to get John's room number. Her heels clacked loudly down a long corridor that smelled of antiseptic. Lou only hoped no one would be in John's room. Hopefully, if she remembered correctly, he wasn't bald and red-faced, but on the other hand, even if he was as homely as Lizzie, apparently dowdiness and scaredy-cat behaviour would win a lot of approval from the TV viewers. Lou needed to get John alone, and when she peeked into the room, she could see him on his back with a drip running into his arm, and the usual monitors beeping and displaying his heart rate and other vitals. "Hi," she said, stepping inside. "How are you, John?"

John's eyes flashed open, and he looked slightly confused.

"Lou," she said, in case he didn't remember her.

"Oh right, the actress. I'm pretty good and probably will be going home before long."

"Great!" Lou beamed and sat on the edge of his bed, taking his hand, remembering the spark that had been between them. "I've been thinking about you."

He wiggled his eyebrows suggestively, making her grin. "Look John, I have a great idea, but you'll have to keep it a secret."

"What's that?"

"How would you like to be on Second Chance Saloon? We need to choose the next guy, and I'd love it to be you."

"I don't know, Lou. I'm pretty weak and will need time to regain my strength."

"Of course," Lou murmured in a gentle conciliatory way. She wasn't an actress for nothing. "But you'd be such a hit, and I could pair you with Cathy or maybe we'd get another woman entirely. A beautiful one. Maybe rich."

"How soon would you need me to appear?"

"How about next week, but of course if it's too much for you, I'll find another man." She moistened her lips seductively.

John half-laughed. "Honestly, Lou, I'm flattered, but I just don't think I'll be well enough."

Lou's heart sank; she'd known it was a long shot but the thought of getting up Charlotte's perfect upturned nose had been too irresistible.

"Sorry, but if I can make it, I will." He shrugged.

"Just, not a word to Charlotte, okay?" Lou tapped the side of her nose as John smiled and nodded in agreement. Lou's phone buzzed with a message. She knew who it was, and said her goodbyes to John, and without looking, hurried outside.

Sweetheart, her lover messaged. *I'll stop by at around eight. I have something important to tell you.*

"No, no no," she mouthed, knowing that if she saw him, any resolve to end their relationship would disappear.

Chapter Twenty

Cathy

Cathy winced as she gently lowered herself onto the couch. Despite the pain medication the doctor had prescribed when she was discharged from the hospital a week ago, she still felt the slight twinge from the scar left by the operation to remove her ovary.

Picking up the remote control, she flicked the TV on, noting from the time on the cheap plastic wall clock that Second Chance Saloon would be starting soon.

She sighed. What a mess that was turning out to be for Lou. What with Lizzie melting down, and then somehow doing a three-sixty turnaround on her second stint, then Charlotte was supposedly appearing, now she wasn't; it was on and off again. Goodness, it was difficult to keep up. Poor Lou, she must be having kittens, Cathy thought, smiling wryly at her feline pun. Coincidentally, Molly, her blue grey, took that moment to jump up on the sofa beside her, curling up with her tail tucked around her, purring softly.

Cathy stroked her head, enjoying the gentle calming of Molly's purr.

"Sweet girl," she cooed, "always there for Mummy, hey?"

She scratched the cat behind the ears, tears suddenly smarting her eyes.

Trouble is that a cat is all that's here for me. That's what my life has come to: a useless piece of flesh, with half my womanly organs gone; fat, old and unattractive.

Cathy wiped an indulgent tear from her cheek and turned her attention back to the TV.

Wait! What the heck? Was that...? Oh my, Lou had really gone and done it now!

58

Tears and self-pity forgotten, Cathy stared open-mouthed at the screen, as a garishly dressed Lou, in a bright pink jumpsuit, introduced the new contestant, John, hailing from the States and a little frail due to a recent surgical procedure.

"Welcome John, such a pleasure to have you join us…"

Cathy jumped as her mobile suddenly trilled and she wasn't surprised to see who was calling.

She picked up the device and swallowed, steeling herself for the diatribe she expected.

"Hello Charlotte," she mumbled.

"Did you know?" Charlotte wailed down the phone.

Cathy shook her head, then realising that of course Charlotte couldn't see her, "No, I didn't…"

"I can't believe Lou has done this. I was happy to go on the show, finally persuaded myself it was time to move on, and what does she do? Brings bloody John, my ex-husband on the show!"

"Well, I…" Cathy tried to interject but Charlotte hadn't finished.

"And John, what the hell is he thinking? He's not long out of hospital, supposed to be resting! Well, if he's well enough to go flaunting himself on a dating show, he can darn well look after himself when he gets back here. I'm done!"

Cathy, though in agreement with Charlotte, felt a little hurt that she hadn't yet asked how she, Cathy, was doing after her procedure. It was unlike the usually polite and considerate Charlotte she was used to, but maybe that was a measure of just how mad she was right now.

"I'm not sure, but I don't think Lou has as much power over the show as she might like to admit…" Cathy tried tentatively.

"But how would anyone else know John: he didn't apply, he's not even a resident here! It must have been Lou, who else?"

Cathy nodded to herself. She had to concede Charlotte had a point. And Lou was well known for her penchant for putting the cat amongst the pigeons so…

"Oh, Cathy," Charlotte was suddenly calmer, "I'm so sorry, I didn't ask how you are, in all my annoyance. Are you all out of pain now?"

Cathy smiled, there she was, the sweet Charlotte she was used to.

As she updated her friend on her health, her eyes were on the TV screen, where Lou had a heavily ringed hand on John's thigh, leaning into him, a seductive smile on her bright pink lips.

What is she up to? Cathy mused. Did she want John for herself? If so, surely setting him up as a contestant on a dating show wasn't the way to go about it. And how would that affect the dynamics of her friendship with Charlotte if she were successful?

Tuning back into the conversation with Charlotte, Cathy felt her heart sink. No doubt about it, change was afoot in this strange friendship group that was their book club.

Cathy didn't much like change, especially since the ending of her relationship so long ago, not something she cared to dredge up or even think about.

Chapter Twenty-One

Victoria

"Good to see you, Victoria." Lou gushed. "I have a wonderful surprise for you!"

Victoria nodded her head, wishing she'd never agreed to come on the show. What had she been thinking? But she wouldn't sink Lou's show by being inappropriate. She stared at her knees covered by wide grey linen trousers. She'd debated about linen knowing it could get creased and wrinkled very easily, but hey that was the style. She, unlike Lou in a revealing tight red top, was wearing an oversized tunic that fell below her waist. Navy blue. At least she felt smart and not tarty.

"So," Lou said with a big grin on her face, looking directly into the camera, and speaking into the overhead boom that reminded Victoria of an upside down Busbee helmet. "So, my book club friend here with us today was reluctant to come on the show. But she is going to be so happy in spite of her misgivings!"

Victoria's jaw dropped.

Lou smiled at her. "So, Vic, what were you worried about?"

Victoria was tempted to tell her the truth, that she considered Lou a cat, but not a good one with fur like her Biscuit. She managed to bite her tongue before saying, "we all deserve a second chance, Lou."

"Indeed! Tell me about your ex. What did he look like?"

"Looks aren't everything and don't matter to me. Loyalty and friendship do."

"Did he cheat on you?"

Victoria slowly got on her feet, ready to walk off the set. She had no intention of being made a fool off by the likes of Lou or anyone else.

"Please stay," Lou said, looking contrite, but Victoria realised she was probably acting, and she was not going to play along. "I'm sorry," she muttered, "but this interview is over."

"Wait!" Lou cried. "I have a wonderful match for you. His name is John. He is
handsome, not to mention kind. You must give him a chance."

Yankee Doodle Dandy sounded, and on limped John, leaning on a cane. He smiled at Lou and grinned at Victoria before managing to sit on a firm chair, letting his stick fall down.

Victoria glared at Lou. *Surely*, she thought, *Lou wasn't really setting her up with Charlotte's ex.* "Maybe *you* are the one who should give this guy a second chance," she said shrewdly, before sitting back down. "But of course, I'd love to meet *your* John."

Lou's smug face underneath her pancake heavy makeup was no doubt turning red. "Oh no," she mouthed. "I have my man."

Just then, a tall guy, a well-known character actor, strode into the room and air-kissed Lou. "I am so glad Lou. You deserve the best!"

Lou frowned and was obviously flustered and at a loss for words.

"Cut!" the director instructed.

Victoria was escorted from the room and asked to wait while things were sorted out. She felt like leaving but sank into a plush sofa and stared at a beautiful landscape painting on the opposite wall. A few moments later, John hobbled out of the set and sat down next to her.

Victoria drew back and wrapped her arms around herself.

John chuckled. "I don't bite, Victoria."

"Well, you certainly sunk your teeth into Charlotte!" Victoria retorted, feeling furious with the events that had just unfolded. *What a farce of a show!*

"What about it?" John replied. "Charlotte and I have been over for a very long time. I'm allowed a second chance too."

Before Victoria could answer, loud voices silenced them, and they both began listening.

"What are you doing here, Richard?" Lou shouted.

"I wanted to surprise you," the man answered. "I went to your flat and heard someone moving about. Obviously not your cat." He chuckled. "I'm happy for you and I hope you'll be happy for me. I am moving to the

States."

"What!" Lou cried. "What about your wife?" Lou's voice was high and strained.

"I'm leaving her. I've met someone."

Lou gasped. "How could you!" she cried.

"I owe you nothing, Lou. We've had a good time over the years."

"Get out," Lou screamed. "Get off my set, you creep!"

"Hey," Richard said. "It's thanks to me you are even on a set. I pulled some strings for you to get this gig. Try to be grateful."

Victoria was suddenly glad to be done with all men as she watched this Richard guy stride past her to the exit. What a jerk! She'd much rather live with Biscuit. But she could hear Lou crying and, against her better judgement, felt sorry for her. She went onto the set, where the cameras had now paused, and the director was spitting feathers and flailing his arms in anger and wrapped her arms around the sobbing Lou. "Hush, Lou," she murmured. "You deserve better," she said, hoping it wasn't a lie.

John approached them, trying to wrap his arms around them both, obviously needing them to help hold him upright.

"For God's sake, John," Victoria spat. She took his arm and led him to a chair.

"You really do deserve a decent man, Vicky," John said, winking as he cheekily shortened her name.

Lou faced the director. "I quit!" she wailed.

Victoria heard the whir of the camera and realised they were being filmed again. She certainly did not want to be part of this kind of reality TV that exposed people's past behaviour, but maybe... "Don't give up your show, Lou!" Victoria was suddenly centre stage. "It doesn't matter how you were selected. Tell your audience what's going on with this guy. Let people know how you've been hurt and that you'd like a second chance, too, with someone trustworthy and decent." As Victoria uttered these words, she knew it was true for her too.

"Like me," John piped up.

"Shut up, John!" Victoria instructed.

John shrugged and hauled himself out of the chair, grabbed his cane and shuffled off the set.

Lou wiped her eyes and began to talk into the camera, pouring out lost years of hopes and dreams with a married man who'd used her with no intention of ever marrying her. It was an old, old story, but Victoria's heart softened towards Lou who was suffering the loss of a false dream. She didn't feel much different but at least she hadn't led Lizzie on. Victoria also realised she'd never been able to please her ex-husband because she'd never really been in love with him, just the idea of it. Her marriage had been a way to cover up her true feelings and look respectable. Really, she'd led *him* on. Gosh, she was no better than the creepy actor guy. "Don't give up, Lou," she murmured under her breath, no longer wanting the spotlight on her. "We'll both get a second chance that will make us everlastingly happy."

Chapter Twenty-Two

Charlotte

Charlotte stared open-mouthed at the TV, unable to believe what she had just witnessed. First, the fact that Victoria had agreed to be on the show had, in itself, blown her mind. The stern no-nonsense Victoria who had not an ounce of patience or care for the whimsical Lou? Second, that some actor guy had gate-crashed the set, in full camera view, to tell Lou, who it turned out had been screwing the guy for decades, he'd finally left his wife. But not for the patiently waiting Lou, but for somebody else entirely!

Could things get any crazier? Charlotte mused.

And would the show get cancelled, or Lou fired? If so, I guess there goes my second chance.

Sinking back into the sofa with a sigh, Charlotte also considered John. Why was Lou keen to set Victoria up with John? It was clear Lou had a thing for him herself, so what was she playing at? It made Charlotte more than glad she was no longer married to him. Once a philanderer, always one, she thought.

The sudden ringing of the house phone made her jump almost out of her seat, so rare was it in these days of mobile phones for a call to actually come in on the landline.

Figuring it would be a tele-sales call, Charlotte let it ring through to voicemail and got up to go into the kitchen. She needed a steadying glass of wine after watching the carnage of tonight's show, then perhaps she'd call Lizzie and see if she'd heard from Victoria or Lou.

Opening the fridge, she pulled out an opened bottle of her favourite Sauvignon Blanc, pausing as she heard the beep of her answerphone.

Grabbing a glass from the cupboard, half listening to the message being left, she stopped at the sound of a once familiar voice.

"Charlotte, it's me, love, I'm so sorry. I can explain, I'm okay, I just..."

There followed an inaudible muffled sound, as Charlotte stood rigid.

"...to contact...but you...trying to...couldn't find..."

"Colin!" Charlotte gasped, as the wine bottle crashed to the floor, followed swiftly by her fainting form.

She didn't know how long she'd been out, but a frantic voice got her attention.

"Mom, wake up, Mom!"

Charlotte opened her eyes, trying to focus on the concerned face of her daughter, Sue.

"What happened?" she gently asked as she helped her sit up from her position on the kitchen floor.

She shook her head, blinking several times to clear her vision.

"I, I don't know..."

"Here, drink this," Sue filled a cup with water and handed it to her, placing a hand on her forehead.

Charlotte sipped gratefully, suddenly realising how dry her mouth was.

"Come on, let's get you on the sofa."

Sue carefully helped her up and with her arms around her, she guided her into the living room. Charlotte couldn't help thinking how times had changed; once she'd have been the one with the steadying arms around her child, and now Sue, a grown woman, was caring for her.

"Thanks, honey." Charlotte relaxed into the seat and closed her eyes again, willing Sue not to ask again what had happened, because she still couldn't quite believe it herself.

Had she imagined it? Was that really Colin she had heard, after all these years? She needed to check the message again and couldn't do that with Sue here.

"I'm fine, honestly." She assured Sue as she sat next to her, worry etched on her lovely face.

"What happened? Are you ill?"

Charlotte quickly shook her head no.

"I didn't eat much today, is all. Must be low blood sugar..."

Before she could finish, Sue was up on her feet.

"I'll make you an omelette!"

"No, Sue, please, it's fine." She was thankful for her daughter's caring nature, but she really needed her to go so she could listen to the message again.

"Mom, I insist on getting you something to eat! I'm not leaving till you've eaten and I'm sure you're okay."

Charlotte sighed and resigned herself to the situation. Sue wasn't going to give up, so the sooner she ate something, reassured her she was ok, the sooner she would go.

And the sooner she could hear Colin again.

Chapter Twenty-Three

Victoria

The book club women had all shown up when Victoria invited them, even Lizzie, thank God, who looked smug. It rankled Victoria but she wouldn't be petty about Lizzie's boyfriend, Bill. The idea of a boyfriend turned her stomach. She settled the women in with glasses of wine in her special crystal, noting Charlotte's red eyes and wondering if John had gone back to the States. Lou didn't look any worse than her usual garish self and certainly didn't look red-eyed, so maybe she'd gotten over the bombshell that had been dropped on her, and maybe the show was still going to be on the air. Cathy was her usual quiet self but had obviously bought some new clothes and looked quite pretty. It was too bad she had such low self-esteem.

Before Victoria had a chance to talk—her plan being to reveal that she was gay—Charlotte, in a high voice, got their attention. "Girls, I need your help. Colin left me a message. I can't believe it."

"How do you know it was him?" asked Lizzie.

Charlotte shrugged. "It sounded like his voice."

"Did you call him back?" Lou asked.

"I tried." She took her phone out of her handbag and stared at it.

"What happened?" Lizzie muttered.

"He wasn't there," Charlotte burst into tears, and they all hushed with concerned looks on their faces. "A woman answered the phone!" Charlotte bawled.

"That rat!" Lou said.

"I wonder what he wanted?" said Lizzie.

"I don't know, and I don't care," Charlotte asserted, wiping her eyes with the tissue provided by Victoria.

"Do you have the phone number," Lou asked. "Let's call again and find out what's going on."

"I can't," Charlotte mumbled.

"Give me your phone," Lou demanded and snatched it from Charlotte's hand.

"No don't," Charlotte moaned, "I can't stand it!"

Lou paid no attention and hit the redial button and turned on the speaker so everyone could hear. A woman's voice answered. "Hello," she said, sounding Scottish. "How may I help you?"

"This is Lou, a friend of Colin's. Might I speak with him?"

"Too late. He checked out yesterday afternoon."

"Checked out," Victoria mouthed. "What does that mean?"

"Surely not!" said Cathy, obviously painfully aware of her once precarious diagnosis and subsequent surgery.

"Excuse me," Lou continued speaking into the phone. "Is this a hotel?"

"This is a B & B. As for Colin, he only stayed a couple of days. Furthermore, he used my landline without permission and needs to pay for the call."

"Where are you located?" Charlotte asked.

"Inverness in the Highlands."

"Do you know where Colin was going?"

"I don't, and even if I did, I couldn't reveal confidential information about my guests." With that, she hung up.

They stared at one another, unable to say a word until Lou took a loud slurp from her wine glass and then refilled all their glasses. "You know," she said. "I've always fancied a trip to the Highlands."

Charlotte threw her a sideways glare. "He will probably call again," she remarked. "Unless he shows up at my house." She held her head between her hands. "Oh God! John is there still. What will Colin think?"

Cathy surprised them by answering wisely, "It doesn't matter what he does or does not think. He's been gone for years. You might have had many new men since him. He owes you an explanation."

Lou grimaced. "He must want something. What a creep!"

"Maybe not," Victoria intervened. "Why don't we book this B & B and go find out for ourselves more about Colin and where he might have gone?"

"I can't go. I've got my show to host." Lou shrugged as the other ladies glanced at each other; they still had no answers as to the fallout for Lou after the last episode, and Charlotte shook her head. She, more than most, had questions for Lou after the debacle she created with John's appearance, but now was not the time.

Lizzie looked down. "And I've got Bill to think about. We're dating now, you know."

"We do know,' Victoria cried, "but we're in this together." She took the phone from Lou and hit the redial.

They listened to the phone ringing and the same Scottish woman answered. "How might I help you?" she said politely, obviously unaware this call was from the same line as before.

"Hello," Victoria said. "My girlfriends and I are planning an all-girls' weekend. Might you have rooms for five of us? And what are your rates?"

"I have two doubles and could pull out a rollaway for the fifth one of you. Since there's five of you and you'll need both my rooms, I'll give you my best rate, which includes breakfast. How does seventy pounds per room per night sound? When do you want to come?"

"We were hoping to come this weekend. Are your rooms available and if so, could you give us directions, please?"

"It so happens, I had a cancellation, so both rooms will be free. Where will you be coming from?"

"We'll probably fly in from London," Victoria answered and then jotted down the directions and hung up. "We could drive," she remarked.

There was silence.

"It's impossible," Lou remarked. "If it *was* your Colin, Charlotte, he might be anywhere by now."

"I know," Charlotte moaned. "I've waited and hoped for three years for him to come back or contact me and now that he has, I don't want him to disappear again. I want to and need to know what's going on. If he doesn't call me or, God help me, show up before the weekend, I want to go." She stared at each of the women, one by one. "*And* I need your support. I want you all to come with me."

70

Chapter Twenty-Four

Charlotte

"Please hurry, I can't hold it in anymore!" Cathy's pleading tone from the passenger seat made Lou chuckle.

"Engage the pelvic floor, Doll!"

"I'm going as fast as I can within the legal limit," Victoria commented dryly. "I'll turn off at the next services."

Charlotte sighed and closed her eyes. Perhaps this wasn't such a good idea after all, inviting the cat ladies along. She already felt exhausted after just three hours with them in the six-seater hire car Victoria had rented, and they'd only been on the M6 for one of them!

"Just don't think about dripping taps or flowing rivers," Lou chided, a twinkle in her eye.

"Stop!" Cathy and Victoria screamed in unison, as Lou cackled away to herself.

Charlotte glared at Lou, annoyed to see a slight smirk on her heavily made-up face.

"We need to have a plan for when we get there," Victoria eyed Charlotte in the rear-view mirror.

Charlotte nodded and Lou sat forward from the back seat, peering into the middle row. "We'll ask around the area, there must be a local pub or village shop that Colin would have visited. Somebody must have seen him or spoken to him."

The other four women nodded in agreement, except for Cathy whose lips were tightly closed and her legs tightly crossed.

"That's actually a good idea, coming from you," Victoria noted, and Lou huffed but didn't rise to the bait.

"He may even have left a forwarding address or phone number at the B&B, maybe there's some way we could get it off the landlady." Lizzie turned to Charlotte.

"The thing is…" Charlotte spoke quietly, deep in thought for a moment. "What exactly am I hoping for if I do find him?"

"Let's not worry about that until it happens," Lizzie comforted her.

"Well, it'd better bloody happen!" Lou chipped in. "I'm already in dire straits with the production company. This could be the straw that breaks the camel's back, me skipping off to Scotland on a whim."

Charlotte sighed and rolled her eyes at Lizzie, who intervened.

"We're all giving something up, Lou, to help a friend. Have some compassion."

"Quite." Charlotte looked at Lou sternly, "and don't think you're getting away without explaining to me your intentions with John, but that can wait for now, I guess."

Lou had the good grace to blush and sat back grumpily in her seat.

"Please, how long Victoria, I'm literally going to…" Before Cathy could finish her beseeching sentence, Victoria suddenly shouted.

"Services! Three miles! Hold on, Cathy, we're almost there."

Lizzie, Charlotte and Lou all smiled.

"Pelvic floor…" murmured Lou, "pelvic floor…"

As the services appeared like a beacon on the long dark stretch of the M6, the others began to chime along with Lou.

"Pelvic floor, pelvic floor…"

"Stop, don't make me laugh!" Cathy gasped as Victoria clicked the indicator to turn off into the service station.

Pulling into a vacant spot in the vast car park, Victoria had barely pulled the hand brake up before Cathy was out of the car and racing to the entrance in an ungainly fashion, as the four other ladies howled in amusement.

Maybe, thought Charlotte, *this was just the kind of bonding trip we needed.*

Chapter Twenty-Five

Cathy

Had she known how long this drive to Inverness was going to be, even with all five of them insured to take turns driving, she wouldn't have come. At least she didn't have to do any driving, since Victoria did the lion's share, with Charlotte and Lou taking turns. So here they were, almost in Inverness, and even though it was already 6 o-clock, it was still light so they could see pretty flowers in gardens, and thank God, it wasn't raining. She'd heard April could be brutal up here in Scotland and at times there could be snow.

Charlotte was fiddling with the Satnav, putting in the address of the B & B, and Victoria was confidently obeying its directions. Soon they were pulling into the driveway of a pretty white croft cottage with upstairs dormers. Cheerful golden daffodils were blooming all along the front of the house.

As they were climbing out of their car, the front door opened and a matronly woman with grey hair pulled into a bun waved to them. "I'm Ruthie. Do you need help with your luggage, ladies?" she asked pleasantly, welcoming them.

"We've got everything, thanks," Lou responded.

"Would you like some sandwiches, or did you eat on your way?"

"We got some fast food so we're good." Lizzie said, smiling.

Soon, Ruthie showed them the upstairs bedrooms they would be sharing. The first room had a queen bed and an ensuite. "Two of you can share the bed, and one of you can have the rollaway in the corner. The other room has two twins. I hope that will suit you."

Cathy could see Victoria looking dubiously at the queen and guessed she didn't want to share with Lizzie. "I'll take the rollaway," she said quickly.

"And I'll sleep in a twin single in the other room." Lizzie replied, equally fast.

"Well," Lou remarked, "Charlotte, how about we share this luxurious queen?" She sunk onto the mattress and patted the spot next to her. Charlotte grimaced but nodded her assent.

Cathy grinned. "I'll be happy to sleep in the other room with Lizzie. I prefer my own bed."

"You're all set then," Ruthie intervened. "I serve breakfast at eight if that's okay. Full Scottish with haggis, and some of our fine ham from a local farm."

"Sounds delicious," Cathy remarked.

"I do my best. And there is a hot tub in the back of the house overlooking the River Ness if you care to use it." Ruthie quietly took her leave.

"I didn't bring a bathing suit," fussed Lizzie.

"Who cares!" sang Lou, plucking two bottles of wine out of her carryall case. "We can go au naturel or you can keep your knickers on."

Lizzie looked pale but clearly wasn't going to object.

"Meet you in the tub in an hour," Lou said. "Someone fetch some glasses from the kitchen."

"I'll get them," Charlotte responded, "but I don't think we can take actual glass ones into the hot tub. Hopefully, they'll be some plastic ones, or paper cups."

"Whatever!"

It was seven o'clock by the time they all arrived at the tub which was set up on a wooden deck a hundred yards or so from a gently flowing river. Cathy felt a bit embarrassed about her saggy underwear, especially seeing Lou's matching lacy black bra and skimpy panties. Lizzie wore plain white cotton knickers and a sad-looking bra that was probably a hundred years old. She at least was not particularly vain. Victoria was wearing a long t-shirt that drooped down to her knees. Cathy hated to have to tell her that once it was wet, everything was going to show, including her nipples that were already rigid from the chilly air. Charlotte sat a handful of paper cups on a nearby table. "Brr," she muttered, and quickly climbed into the hot tub before anyone could pay much attention to her respectable but not particularly sexy lingerie.

Soon, they'd downed their first bottle of wine and were chatting away gaily. The second bottle quickly disappeared too. And Lizzie, to everyone's surprise, rushed out of the steamy water and came back with two more bottles of Pinot Grigio.

"I didn't think you drank much," Victoria remarked.

"Bill is introducing me to all sorts of things I've never done before."

"I bet!" Lou cackled.

Cathy could see Lizzie's face turning red in the overhead fairy lights. "A little wine is good for your health," she said. "But I think we ought to get some snacks, or we'll be a mess tomorrow when we go looking for Colin."

"We need to ask Ruthie about his stay here," Charlotte said quietly. "Maybe she can point us in the right direction. Or maybe he had to sign in and she has an address."

"That makes sense," Victoria said. "I looked up Inverness and at least fifty thousand people live here."

After a while, Ruthie appeared through a sliding glass door that led onto the deck from the lounge. She smiled. "I brought you some towels."

"You are so kind," Cathy said. "Why don't you join us for a glass of wine?"

"Oh, I don't know. I don't want to intrude on your hen club."

"We wish you would," Charlotte remarked. "We are here for more than a girls' weekend. Colin, who was staying here, is my husband. He disappeared three years ago and never sent any word until he rang me from here. I'm sorry we didn't explain that was the reason we were coming. My friends are with me to support me. I am hoping to find him again. It's been an agony, almost like a death, only worse because there's no finality and no closure."

"Oh, dearie me." Ruthie got a stricken look on her face. "I recently lost my husband. He fell over and died from a heart attack. I've been angry with him, especially since our move here to open this B & B was our dream, and now I'm stuck doing it all by myself."

"I feel like a prune," Lou said, climbing out of the tub and wrapping herself in a towel. "Let's go in where it's warm."

"I'll get a fire going in the hearth, ladies, and I'll get you some snacks. And we can talk."

They were soon gathered around a roaring fire with mugs of hot chocolate warming their hands. "Ruthie," Charlotte said. "You are a darling. Did Colin leave any kind of address or tell you anything that might help me find him?"

"Jerk that he is," Lou stated, a rim of frothy hot chocolate sticking to her upper lip.

"He signed the register and gave me his license plate number but that's about it. The only thing I remember him saying was he wanted to visit Nairn beach by the North Sea and watch the dolphins."

Chapter Twenty-Six

Charlotte

The thirty-minute drive to Nairn beach was bittersweet.

Lou, nursing a hangover, had offered to drive, but no-nonsense Victoria absolutely put pay to that; "You're probably still over the limit, absolutely not!"

Lou had chuckled as she fell into the back seat, gracing the other ladies with the whiff of her still wine-fuelled breath.

Ever kind Lizzie patted Charlotte's knee. "How're you feeling?"

Charlotte smiled sadly, "Nervous?"

Victoria glanced at her in the rearview mirror, her hands steady on the wheel. "Why nervous? If it were me, I'd be champing at the bit to find the cad and give him a piece of my mind!"

"Ha! Why doesn't that surprise me?" Lou scoffed from the back, smirking at the tut-tut response from Victoria.

"I think Charlotte needs to know why he disappeared before making judgements and getting cross with Colin," Lizzie diplomatically said.

Charlotte nodded, pensively.

"You know what, though? I *am* angry at him. Yes, of course, I need to hear him out, to find out what happened with him. But I've put my life on hold for the last few years. I deserve to know the truth, it's just…"

The other ladies listened, waiting.

"Just what?" Lou finally asked into the silence.

Charlotte closed her eyes and turned her face upwards. "It's just, what if the truth hurts?"

Victoria gripped the steering wheel tighter. "What could possibly hurt more than not knowing?"

"Knowing he left her for another woman?" Lou suggested,

unhelpfully.

"Lou!" Cathy and Lizzie groaned in unison and Victoria shook her head.

"What?" Lou exclaimed. "I'm just putting it out there!"

"As always." Victoria replied haughtily, which, even in her pensive mood, made Charlotte smile.

Fortunately, they arrived at the beach minutes later; its sandy stretch eclipsed by the pretty promenade overlooking the Moray Firth.

Charlotte breathed out deeply. "This is simply stunning."

The other ladies murmured their agreement as they unfolded themselves out of the car.

"I can see exactly why Colin would want to come here," Charlotte wiped a tear from her eye.

"Come on, Doll, we'll get to the bottom of this." Lou placed an uncharacteristically comforting arm around Charlotte's shoulders, and she leaned in gratefully.

"Yes, we will," Victoria chipped in, determinedly. "So, ladies, what now?"

"Find a bar?" Lou sniggered, back to her normal self, as Victoria rolled her eyes.

"Let's just walk along the beach for a while, maybe." Charlotte held a hand above her eyes, looking out at the vast expanse of sand. "Colin wasn't a big drinker; I doubt he'd be in a bar. He'd most likely be poking around looking for sea life." She smiled wistfully.

"Come on," Cathy took Charlotte's hand, "let's go look for our own type of sea life."

Charlotte giggled but followed Cathy's lead.

"So, no bar then," Lou grumbled from behind as they began to trudge along the sand.

Chapter Twenty-Seven

Charlotte

As they trudged along with their heads down against the wind coming off the sea, Charlotte felt as grey as the clouds that were threatening a downpour, but the roaring of the ocean, rolling whitecaps and the salty air curling her hair made her smile. She remembered how her kids loved their holidays at Myrtle Beach and how they'd scream as soon as they caught sight of the Atlantic. This North Sea, though, was a lot wilder and colder. Maybe, she speculated, she ought to go back to the States and be closer to her kids.

They were the only people on the beach, probably because of the threat of storms, plus it was only around ten in the morning. Ruthie at the B & B had laid out quite a spread for breakfast: scrambled eggs, bacon, sausages, baked beans, fried bread, toast, marmalade, jam, and pots of strong tea. She'd even insisted on lending Charlotte the yellow slicker she was wearing and had apologised she didn't have raincoats for all of them which they were going to need as big drops of rain began to splatter onto the sand.

"Quick," Victoria grabbed Charlotte's hand and dragged her towards a beach café with outside seating and, fortunately, inside tables too.

Once they'd settled inside, on a bench table overlooking the water, a friendly young Scot with reddish hair and a warm smile brought them steaming hot coffees and suggested pastries. "No thanks, darling," Lou flirted.

Charlotte noticed Victoria shaking her head. What on earth was she, Charlotte, doing with these crazy women? She held her mug of coffee in her hands to warm them and found herself giving all the cat ladies descriptive adjectives. There was Caring Cathy, the former nurse, who always wanted to make things better. And Lizzie was, well lucky, now that she'd found Bill, so Lucky Lizzie it was. And luscious or should it be lascivious Lou? Poor woman was a mess really and obviously lonely and unfulfilled; her irrational plan of bringing John onto her show had proven that. Charlotte took a sip of coffee and peeked at Victoria over the rim. Veiled Vicky, she thought, realising that Victoria thought no one knew she was gay and though the women never talked about it, everyone knew! In the hot-tub, Charlotte thought Victoria was about to come out when she whispered she had something important to tell them, but they'd been interrupted by Ruthie with the towels. It must be difficult to hide your true identity. She needed an adjective to describe herself: I am Clever Charlotte. After all, I am a professor and teach students and have a good job. But how smart am I really? What am I doing on this wild goose chase?

She knew for sure it had been Colin who'd called, but what did he expect after all these years? And where had he been? She'd once thought maybe he'd been kidnapped by pirates, but no ransom money was ever demanded, and she didn't think he'd been near the North Sea on his last marine expedition. It could have been amnesia, but Caring Cathy had told her on their trip up the motorway that it was unlikely for amnesia to last years. A terrible idea came into her mind: what if he'd committed a heinous crime and been in prison, but she couldn't imagine her nerdy husband as an axe murderer. The most likely explanation was another woman, and he had certainly charmed the panties off her. She groaned to herself, realising how needy she had been, even though she'd supported herself, survived a divorce and raised her kids successfully. Did she even want Colin back or was that a futile fantasy? She had no answer but maybe if she saw him and he explained himself, their feelings of love might be restored.

Outside, dark clouds rolled in from the sea and rain began pounding down, scattering all the seagulls. Where did the birds go to get out of the weather, she wondered, but of course they had waterproof feathers. It surprised her to see a tall thin man jogging past as if he hadn't a care in the world. What a fool! she thought. But as he raced past the window, and she caught a better glimpse of him, she thought he could actually be Colin. Running in the rain was just the sort of thing he might do. She gasped and jumped up from her seat, rushing to the front door. The other women were right behind her.

The rain lashed onto the patio and Charlotte pulled the hood up on her yellow slicker. "Colin!" she screamed at the man's back. "Colin!" The wind, the rain, the loud waves swamped out her voice, but the ladies all joined in. "Colin," they yelled, their voices drowned by thunder followed by jagged bolts piercing the sea.

"Ladies," the young waiter called from inside the entranceway to the café, "Come back in. It's dangerous to be on the beach in this weather. You could get struck by lightning!"

Charlotte paid no attention to him. She could barely see the man through the rain, but she was determined to find out if he was, in fact, Colin. She began yelling again, "Colin, come back!" The others joined their voices with hers. She distinctly heard one of them scream, "you creep, get back here!"

If in the unlikely event he heard them, he didn't stop. If anything, he seemed to be running faster. Running away, Charlotte thought, and dashed into the weather, her yellow slicker flapping wildly against her legs. The other women rushed after her. Victoria led the pack, with Lizzie belting along next to her doing her best to catch up on her short legs. Cathy, not fully recovered from surgery, lagged behind, gasping for breath. Lou brought up the rear. Charlotte, in that wild moment, realised what good friends they were and hesitated long enough for them to catch up. They were like an army unit in hot pursuit of an enemy. Charlotte didn't know whether to laugh or cry. But first they needed to get hold of this idiot who they could hardly see now but looked as if he was running for his life. Maybe he was!

Chapter Twenty-Eight

Lou

Lou swallowed back hysterical giggles as she gave chase along with the other cat ladies. *What must they look like? A gaggle of middle-aged women chasing a random man in the sheeting rain!*

As Victoria yelled out that he was a creep, Lou allowed the giggle to burst from her throat, not missing the side eye she received from Victoria in return.

As they raced to keep up with Charlotte, who was a woman on a mission, her usual grace and elegance abandoned as she raced after the would-be Colin, Lou wondered what on earth would happen should they catch up with him and it wasn't Colin!

But wait, the man was slowing down, Charlotte almost upon him.

"C…C…Colin?" Charlotte's voice quivered with uncertainty, and Lou's heart jumped in her chest. *Dear God, don't tell me it's not him. How embarrassing!*

The man stopped, his head turning to look at the four deranged-looking women now in front of him, the fifth catching up the rear; Cathy's face flushed and sweaty. His mouth dropped open.

"Well?" Victoria demanded, fixing her gaze upon Charlotte. "Is it him?"

Charlotte was frozen, her jaw stiff, little pulse points flickering in her cheeks.

Lou nudged her. "Doll, is it him?"

"Excuse me, can I help yee?" The deep Scottish burr of the man's words gave them their answer, and Lou groaned with embarrassment.

Charlotte's already flushed cheeks burned with humiliation. "I'm so sorry," she mumbled, "I thought you were…" She looked down at the ground, her shoulders sagging with the burden of disappointment.

"She thought you were someone else," Victoria chipped in, her brusque business-like manner on full display.

The man looked at Victoria, then back at Charlotte, the lines in his forehead creasing deeper, confusion writ all over his visage.

"Sorry to disappoint yee, ladies. But we really ought to get in from this wee storm. So, if yee dinnit mind, I'll be on my wee way." He doffed an invisible cap and resumed his jog, leaving the cat ladies in his wake.

"Well!" Lou harrumphed, turning to Charlotte.

"I'm sorry!" She wailed, covering her face with her hands. "I thought it was him, honestly!"

Victoria patted her shoulder, comfortingly. "No harm done," she soothed.

"No harm done?" Lou retorted, ignoring Lizzie who was shaking her head at her in an attempt to quieten her. "No harm done?" Lou repeated. "Cathy almost got a hernia on your bloody wild goose chase!"

"I'm fine, it's fine," Cathy interjected but Lou was on a roll.

"And look," she continued, holding up her shoe and waving it menacingly in the air. "I broke my heel!"

A lone tear rolled down Charlotte's cheek and Lou suddenly felt bad.

"Ah, come here, you daft bird." She pulled Charlotte into her, ignoring the furious glances from the other ladies being cast in her direction. "Sorry, I dinnit mean to be harsh, it was a wee bit naughty of me…"

At Lou's dismal attempt at a Scottish accent, Charlotte's sad tears became those of mirth, her shoulders shaking as she laughed uncontrollably. Even Victoria, Lou noticed, couldn't keep a smile off her usually stern face.

Within seconds, five middle aged ladies, their wet hair stuck to their foreheads, with flushed sweaty faces and soaked-through clothes, held each other as their laughter threatened to drown out the roars of thunder all around them.

They didn't see the man observing them from the little tea shop they had failed to notice as they'd dashed past it on their earlier chase. With a shaking hand, he placed his teacup back on the table and unfolded his Marine Life magazine to hold over his face.

Chapter Twenty-Nine

Cathy

There continued to be loud claps of thunder over the ocean, but the rain stopped.

The five bedraggled women were staring out at the lightning flashing in the sky above the sea when they were surprised by two uniformed police officers, a man and a woman who approached them from the café where they had been enjoying hot coffees before Charlotte set them on a wild goose chase.

"Ladies," the guy said to them, "There's been a complaint against you, and we are taking you into the station for questioning."

"But we haven't done anything!" Cathy moaned in a desperate voice. She looked exhausted, and was soaking wet and dead tired, and couldn't take any more drama.

The female police officer, who did not smile, told her and the others to hold out their hands and she and her partner cuffed them. "Yee have the right to remain silent," the man stated. And the female officer, looking intimidating in her black uniform, nodded. "Aye," she said. "What on earth do you think you're up to out here in this storm? Let's go!" She pushed Cathy ahead of her, and soon they were being marched off the beach and were crammed into the back of a white police van with reflective blue and yellow stripes on the sides.

"We're English," Victoria muttered. "We'll have your badges!"

"So ye think that gives you special privileges," the man muttered. "We'll see about that. It's obvious ye've been up to no good and tried to get out of paying for your drinks as if you are immune to prosecution."

"We *were* going to pay!" Victoria cried indignantly.

Charlotte intervened. "It's my fault. I thought the man jogging on the beach was my former husband and I needed to talk to him."

"Apparently, he didn't need to talk to you. And *you* don't sound English."

"I'm an American but I live in London. I'll be happy to pay our bill. We were on our way back there. We're not criminals."

"This is ridiculous!" Victoria shook her head. "Look at us, we're middle-aged respectable women, for goodness sake!"

"Middle aged women who fled a café without paying." The male officer reminded them with a smirk.

"Don't we have a right to make a call?" Victoria asked, sounding less than her usual confident self.

"Ye have the right to remain silent as I told ye. And yes, ye can call your solicitor."

Cathy began to cry. "We came up here to help our friend whose husband has been missing for three years…" she rambled on between sobs. "Please let us go!" she wailed.

"Ye'll be questioned at the station and if the café owner wants to press charges, we'll go from there. There have been several incidents of payment evasion this morning and you lot have just done exactly that. Ye didna pay your drinks bill!"

After they were crammed into a large interview room with no windows, and a door with a large lock, they were freed of their cuffs. There were not enough chairs for all of them, and the four that were there were bolted to the floor, but Charlotte took Cathy's hand and made her sit.

They'd had to turn in all personal effects, including their phones, but now the female officer handed back one phone. "Ye've been allowed to keep one phone to make a call, and I suggest you make it soon."

"It's yours, Charlotte, thank God," Victoria said with a deep sigh. "We'll have to call Ruthie." She stared at the woman officer. "Ruthie is the owner of the B & B where we're staying. She'll vouch for us."

"Ye've got yourselves into a right mess, haven't you? Not to worry, I'll get you all cups of tea," the officer grinned. "Officially on the house!"

"I'm so sorry. You wouldn't happen to have towels for us to dry ourselves with. Please." Cathy's pleading eyes looked enormous.

"I'll see what I can do." The officer clanked the door shut, secured the lock and hung the key out of reach on a hook on the wall.

Victoria dialled Ruthie who answered on the third ring. "How's it going? Did you find him?"

"We're in jail in Nairn," Victoria answered, and they could hear Ruthie exclaim, "Oh my goodness, what happened!"

"It's a long story but we chased a guy on the beach who it turned out was not Colin."

After a pause, where the others couldn't hear what Ruthie was saying, Victoria pulled a face. "Thanks, Ruthie." She clicked off and turned to the others, "Ruthie is coming now."

They were issued blankets and gratefully wrapped themselves in them.

About half an hour later another police officer arrived and balanced a tray on one arm while she managed to open the door. "Here you go, lasses," she said. "These'll warm you up. I'm Inspector Campbell. So, what were you doing on the beach in the pouring rain? And where were you at seven this morning?"

Ruthie burst into the adjoining room. "They were having breakfast. Full English," she said.

"Well, I did not think any of you looked like hardened criminals. Drink your tea and you're free to go, but make sure you pay for your drinks or we'll re-arrest you."

"Yes Ma'am," Charlotte muttered and added, "we are trying to find my husband, Colin."

"Is he an American too?"

"No, he's English and has been missing for a while but he recently called me from here."

"Oh aye, you don't say. My mother mentioned an English fellow who was looking at properties she was selling. If I'm not mistaken, she said his name was Colin. Colin Jones, I think. He couldn't settle the mortgage on the house he wanted to buy until he talked to his wife…"

"Oh my God!" Charlotte gasped. "That's him!"

Chapter Thirty

Lou

"Well, I'm sorry, Doll, but I'm stuck in Scotland right now. What can I do?"

"Oh Lou," the director's voice was testy, "we have to get the show back on air even if I have to replace you…"

Lou interrupted him. "You can't replace me; I brought you half of the contestants!"

"Lou," his voice was firm, "get the hell back now or we're done."

Lou didn't bother to reply as she heard the call cut dead. She sighed, her head in her hands, as Charlotte walked into Ruthie's kitchen.

"You okay?" Charlotte asked, concerned.

"Probably just lost my job, other than that, just dandy!" Lou sniped back.

"I'm so sorry, Lou." Charlotte sat down next to her at the large kitchen island. "This was a wild goose chase I shouldn't have dragged you into."

Lou shook her head. "It wasn't though, was it?"

Charlotte frowned, not understanding.

"It wasn't a wild goose chase; we know Colin is here." Lou was suddenly animated.

Charlotte frowned; "Well, yes, but…"

"But nothing, Doll! We'll find the bugger, and more than that…" Lou stood up from her stool and began punching her fingers into her phone.

"Wait, what…?" Charlotte crinkled her forehead, just as Victoria walked into the kitchen.

Okay? she mouthed, nodding towards Lou. Charlotte held up her hands and shrugged. "I'm not sure. Lou…"

"Hang up on me again, and you'll lose the show of the century!" Lou screeched into her phone.

Charlotte and Victoria exchanged confused glances as they watched Lou.

"What am I talking about? I've got an absolute exclusive for you. Get the camera crew up here now…"

As realisation dawned on Charlotte's face, Victoria, open-mouthed, placed an arm around her shoulders.

"No, no, no…" Charlotte mumbled.

"Lou, what the heck? No way!" Victoria was aghast. "This is a personal and private matter."

Lou waved their words away as she continued talking into her phone.

Charlotte stared at Victoria. "Surely she's not!" she moaned with a resigned sigh.

Victoria shook her head, echoing Charlotte's sigh as she spoke. "Yes, I think she is."

Lou placed her phone down on the kitchen island with a triumphant bang.

"There you go, Doll. This is happening. We *will* find Colin and furthermore…"

"Furthermore?" Victoria rolled her eyes.

"Furthermore…" Lou continued, ignoring Victoria, "we will film the whole thing."

Charlotte gasped.

"Yes," Lou chuckled and rubbed her hands together gleefully.

"No! Absolutely not!" Victoria faced Lou. "This is Charlotte's business; you can't air it to the public!"

Charlotte groaned as she looked at her phone. "It's too late," she muttered and held her phone up to Victoria.

Victoria looked.

An Instagram post stood out: *Second Chance Saloon – It's Charlotte's turn, but we need to find Colin… Colin is in Scotland, near Nairn beach. #whereiscolin*

"Oh my goodness, Lou, what have you done?" Victoria railed at a

beaming Lou, as the beeps of a thousand comments lit up Charlotte's phone:
#whereiscolin #findcolin #savecharlotte #prayforcharlotte #prayforcolin

Lizzie ran into the kitchen. "Charlotte, what's wrong? You look awful!"

Charlotte covered her eyes for a moment and then showed Lizzie the phone. "Lou thinks she's helping…"

"Lou, what the heck did you do?!"

Chapter Thirty-One

Victoria

Victoria and Charlotte remained in the kitchen with Ruthie who was using oven gloves to take fresh baked bread out of the oven. She sat two crispy brown loaves on cooling racks.

Charlotte's face looked grim, but she managed to smile. "That smells heavenly," she complimented Ruthie.

"Thank you," Ruthie said. "I have an idea. The woman who sold me this house has her estate agency in Nairn. Why don't you ask her if she knows where Colin is staying? I can give you her phone number."

Victoria jumped in before Charlotte could say no. "Give us the address and her name. That television crew won't be here for hours. We've got time to find him, and you can have it out with him privately."

Charlotte shook her head. "I feel like going home to be with Mirabelle. At least she's faithful. I'm not sure I care what happens to Colin."

But Victoria jangled her car keys. "What's her name and address, Ruthie? Write it down, please."

She dragged Charlotte out to the car. "You'll regret it if you don't find out the truth," she said. "Trust me, it's for the best to face things and not hide them. Believe me, I should know."

Charlotte cast a curious eye as Victoria said this, wondering what on earth she meant, but knowing now was not the time to delve further.

After Victoria entered the address in the Satnav, she roared out of the driveway and soon they were hurtling towards Nairn Beach. The Estate Agency was easy to find and there was even a parking spot right outside the door. Victoria quickly maneuverer the car parallel to the path. "You ready?" she said to Charlotte with a determined gleam on her face as she leapt out of the car.

A bell on the door chimed when they opened it and stepped into a small room with photos of houses on the walls behind a table where a stern-looking woman sat with a phone in her hand. She looked up at them. "How may I help you?" She sounded miffed as if they'd interrupted something.

Victoria would not be put off by this snooty bitch. "We are staying at a B & B with Ruthie…"

"Ruthie Bennet! I sold her that house! Isn't it fabulous right on the river?" She was now smiling and clicked her phone off. "I hope everything is going well and you are enjoying your stay there. She is a delightful woman. Such a shame her husband passed too early."

"Everything's okay," Charlotte said quietly. "Ruthie's a great host and the house is great."

"You're American!" said the estate agent lady. "How wonderful. Would this be something to do with Colin?"

Charlotte's jaw dropped open. She was speechless but Victoria chimed in, "Indeed it is. Could you give us his address?"

The lady looked a little doubtful.

"I am his wife," Charlotte said, "but I have not seen him in three years. He recently contacted me, but I didn't have his return number."

Victoria launched into all they knew and what had happened, ending with how they thought they'd found him on the beach.

"Dear me," the estate agent said. "He told me he'd been working on the Great Barrier Reef for the past three years. I'd assumed his American wife, you, were with him. He seemed a decent chap."

"I thought so too. But he never even told me where he was. I've been hoping for years he was ok and would somehow show up." Tears filled Charlotte's eyes.

"That bastard!" Victoria muttered.

"He told me he was engaged in important research to restore corals to the reef. Maybe he simply couldn't give it up," the agent said tactfully.

"My first husband left me for another woman," Charlotte moaned. "It must be something about me that makes men leave."

"Nonsense!" Victoria frowned. "There's nothing wrong with you. And the only way to find out if he's got any excuse, which I doubt, is to go and ask him."

"You're right. He's renting the house he wants to buy once he accesses his bank account." The agent wrote down an address on a scrap of paper and handed it to Victoria. "You didn't get this from me!" With that she ushered them out of the door. "Good luck, ladies!"

"He's after your money, Charlotte, I'll bet," said Victoria.

"There is a bank account in his name that I couldn't retrieve without his username and password." Charlotte looked even more wretched.

"Did you know sex and money are the biggest reasons relationships end?'

Charlotte sighed. "I've heard that. But why didn't he just ask me for the money?"

"It seems to me the question is 'what's he got to hide?'"

Charlotte groaned as they set out.

"Maybe he's gay," Victoria suggested. "People often hide their sexuality."

Charlotte faced Victoria and put her hand over Victoria's on the steering wheel. "It must be excruciating to hide your identity behind a veil of secrecy," she said gently.

Victoria gripped the steering wheel hard and stepped on the accelerator. "It isn't easy," she said. And without so much as a glance at Charlotte added, "I've known I've been different since I was in primary school, you know, gay."

"I thought you might be. But it's nothing to be ashamed of. You are a wonderful person."

"Do the others know?"

Charlotte considered her reply. "They may have an inkling."

Chapter Thirty-Two

Lizzie

Lizzie smiled hearing Bill's comforting voice as he answered her call. "Hey babe, how's it going?"

"Oh, it's absolutely crazy!" Lizzie tapped her nails on the side table. "Lou's decided to air poor Charlotte's dirty laundry for all to see and…"

"Wait, what? Slow down." Bill interrupted. "Lou's done what?"

Lizzie took a deep breath. "Yep, the TV crew are due in a few hours." She heard Bill's intake of breath.

"Wow," he murmured, "that's nuts, even for Lou."

"I know!" Lizzie cried. "Meanwhile, Victoria has dragged Charlotte off to confront Colin and…"

"Colin's the missing dude, right?" Bill was obviously struggling to keep up.

"Yes, except he's not missing now and… Oh Bill, why did I ever agree to come? It's just horrendous." Lizzie shook her head in despair.

"Well, why don't you just come home, honey?"

Bill's question was a reasonable one, and Lizzie paused for thought. "The thing is, we kind of have this unspoken pact."

Bill chuckled lightly. "Unspoken pact?"

Lizzie's heart sank; was he laughing at her?

"Yes," she replied coldly, "It's the cat lady thing. I don't know, it's like we need to stick together, have each other's backs, you know?"

"Like girl code?" Bill asked, and Lizzie didn't think she detected any humour or sarcasm in his tone.

"I guess." Lizzie blew through her pursed lips.

"I just miss you, honey, I wasn't trying to patronise you."

Lizzie couldn't help but smile as an idea formed in her mind.

"Bill, why don't you come here?" she suggested.

"What, with the TV crew about to descend. No bloody way, Liz!"

"But why?" Lizzie pushed. "You and I are already part of the show, we *met* on that damn show!"

"Exactly, we met, job done. We don't need any more airtime!" Lizzie could hear Bill's irritation and rushed to placate him.

"Please Bill. I could do with your support. It might take the heat off Charlotte a little bit, and at the same time give Lou the credit she so desires for the TV show." She waited with bated breath, almost hearing the cogs turning in Bill's mind.

Finally, he spoke. "Look, Liz, I'll come…"

"Yes!" Lizzie blew out a sigh of relief, but Bill wasn't finished.

"I'll come, but only for you. I'm not doing any favours for Lou, and poor Charlotte needs to sort her life out in private, so I won't be a part of any circus that involves her and her missing dude."

"Colin," Lizzie added, unnecessarily. "Thank you, honey. When can you get here?"

"I'll be there tomorrow, just hang in there and try to keep Lou under a tight rein."

Lizzie laughed dryly and Bill had to chuckle back. "See you tomorrow, honey."

Lizzie ended the call and hugged her arms around herself. She couldn't wait to see him again.

Ever since they'd hit it off so well on the show, they'd grown really close. There was just something about him, something that made her feel like she could be her true self. And she was attracted to him, oh how she was attracted to him.

She stretched out on her bed, still clutching her phone, deep in thought. She wished her relationship with Bill hadn't hurt Victoria. She knew Victoria had romantic hopes about her, and, whilst there had been a close connection that she and Victoria had shared, for her it would never be romantic or sexual.

Since Lizzie met Bill though, Victoria had withdrawn from her, and Lizzie hadn't really questioned it or fought it. It made her a little sad and guilty for dropping her friend, but she couldn't forget how Victoria had been so dominating. A trait that had initially made Lizzie feel safe, but that had eventually irritated and stifled her.

Victoria was a very hard character; some might even say cold. But Lizzie knew beneath that veneer lay an insecure and deeply unhappy woman. Having denied her sexuality for years within an unhappy marriage, Victoria, she was sure, would thrive in a happy relationship with a woman.

But that woman wouldn't be Lizzie. No, she was with Bill now; Victoria had to move on.

"Where the hell is she?" Lou's shrieked question from downstairs diverted her thoughts away from Victoria.

She was tempted to get under the covers and pull a blanket over her head, but she slipped off the bed, straightened her skirt and ventured down into the chaos.

Chapter Thirty-Three

Lou

Lou, her jaw tight, staring out the lounge window, barely gave Lizzie a sideways glance, but when Cathy laid a hand on her arm, she turned and glared at Cathy and then at Lizzie.

Cathy stepped away and managed a smile at Lizzie. "So, how's Bill?"

Lou glared at them. "Really, we've got better things to think about rather than moon over some stupid man who probably can't be trusted further than we can throw him, and let's face it he's too big to throw far!"

"That's uncalled for," Cathy scolded.

"You, Lou," Lizzi said through clenched teeth, "are the one who introduced us on your stupid show. And *you* hardly have room to talk, chasing after a married man the way you did. And not to mention inviting Charlotte's ex, John, onto your show. What the hell was that about? At least Bill is kind and smart and, as a matter of fact, will be coming here tomorrow to support me!"

"Dear God," Lou moaned. "You're in love with the dude!"

Lizzie turned red. "So, what if I am! He's even taking care of Tom cat for me."

Lou shrugged. "I'm sorry. I'm just anxious about the crew getting here." She turned and looked out of the window. "Where's our car?" she asked. And it was as if a light dawned in her mind. "Surely Victoria hasn't dragged Charlotte into Nairn."

Ruthie came into the room carrying a tray of teacups, a teapot and milk and sugar. "They did." With an apologetic look at Lou, she continued. "Let's have a cuppa and calm down."

Cathy interjected, "I doubt if they could find Colin anyway."

"They might," Ruthie said. "I gave them the number of my realtor and I called her to let her know they were coming."

"We can't have them warning Colin," Lou muttered. "Give me her number! I'm calling an Uber."

"Wait!" Ruthie said. "Do you really think it's right to interfere?"

"Colin is a creep!" Lou sputtered. "He doesn't deserve to be protected."

"But Charlotte does," Lizzie said. "She is a private person. She'll hate being exposed to the whole world on live television."

Lou sank onto the couch and put her head in her hands. "The crew will be here in a matter of hours."

Ruthie poured them all tea and they sat, sipping, without speaking for a while.

Lou sighed. "Charlotte's daughter, Sue, is taking care of Peregrine for me. She'll hate me!"

"Since when did you care what people thought of you?" Lizzie said, obviously still offended at Lou's earlier remarks about Bill.

"We need to stick together," Cathy interjected. "Ruthie, can we borrow your car and go to Nairn to see if we can find them?"

"Of course," Ruthie agreed. "I'll drive."

Fortunately, when they arrived in Nairn, the real-estate lady was still in her office and gladly gave them Colin's address. His house was easy to find, and Lou was soon striding up to the front door and bashing the knocker and ringing the bell. Clearly no one was home and obviously Victoria and Charlotte weren't there either.

"For God's sake!" Lou cursed in disgust. "Now what?"

"Let's go to that beachside coffee shop and then we'll come back and try again."

Lou scowled. "I doubt we'll be welcome there!"

"Don't worry," Ruthie said. "You paid for your drinks in the end, and he probably won't even recognise you."

Lou straightened up. "He certainly *will* recognise me!" she bragged.

Lizzie groaned but said nothing as they drove to the beach.

The sea was grey but fairly calm as they entered the restaurant opposite it. "Oh my gosh," Cathy said, seeing Victoria and Charlotte sitting in a corner, nursing mugs of chocolate.

Lou marched over to their table. "Have you confronted him yet?" she demanded to know, standing over Charlotte.

Charlotte turned and faced her. "No, "she said. "I'm not ready and I may never be. Maybe I drive men away. After all, John left me for another woman and then blamed me. And Colin seemed so perfect but looking back, I latched onto him because he was English, and I wanted to come to the land of Shakespeare and Keats and Jane Austen."

"Psah!" Lou spat out. "Do not blame yourself! You are not responsible for their behaviour."

The other women were all nodding in agreement as the door opened, letting in a rush of cool, salty air. A tall thin man hesitated in the entrance way.

Chapter Thirty-Four

Charlotte

Charlotte looked up and her jaw stiffened, her eyes filled with terror, and she inhaled sharply.

"What is it?" Victoria looked quickly in the direction of Charlotte's gaze. "Is that him? Is that the coward?" She stood up, her upper lip curling up in a snarl. Lou groaned and fell into the empty seat, her head in her hands.

"Wait, no, Victoria, please don't!" Charlotte stood and grabbed Victoria's arm. "It's not Colin."

Victoria looked at Charlotte, eyebrows raised. "It's not Colin? Then why are you staring at him?"

Lou looked up hopefully. "It's not him? Oh, thank goodness, the show will go on!"

Lizzie tutted and glared at Lou, before turning to Charlotte. "And why is he staring at you?"

Charlotte swallowed. Lizzie was right, the man who had just entered was gazing right into her eyes, drinking her in, and she flushed from her neck upwards.

She wasn't lying when she said it wasn't Colin. It wasn't Colin as she knew him. The Colin she had known, and loved, was a broad handsome man, with ruddy cheeks and a full head of dark wavy hair. This man, who now stood by the café door, was thin, scrawny even, his face pale and gaunt, his clothes hanging off his rail thin body. No, this wasn't her Colin, but technically it *was* Colin.

The man seemed to gather himself, but as he walked timidly towards her, gone was the confident stride he once possessed.

"Charlotte…" His voice was the same, albeit quieter and unsteady.

Lou stood up. "It is him!"

Victoria looked at Charlotte, her eyes wide, confusion masking her face. "Well, Charlotte?"

Charlotte stood up as if to greet the man, but she could feel her legs weakening. "I need to… sit…" For a moment she was suddenly conscious of the stares of the other café customers all transfixed with the scene before them and before she knew it, Charlotte collapsed to the floor, her hearing suddenly muted and everything went black.

"Quick, get her into the chair," Victoria, brisk and organised as ever, bent down to gather Charlotte in her arms. "And water, someone bring her some water."

As the other women bent to help Charlotte, Colin turned to leave.

"And where do you think you're going?" Victoria shouted. "You stay right where you are, you cowardly excuse of a man!"

Colin had the good grace to look embarrassed and shrugged his shoulders helplessly.

"She's coming round." Cathy murmured, her arm around Charlotte's shoulder. "It's okay, you're going to be okay."

Charlotte blinked as Cathy's blurred face floated before her and she brought her hand to her pounding head.

"Are you hurt?" Cathy asked. Charlotte shook her head and winced at the pain. "Just a tension headache." she muttered, then looked up at Colin, hovering nervously behind Victoria.

"Were you going to walk away again, Colin?" she whispered, tears pooling in her eyes.

"I shouldn't have come, I…" He paused, words seemingly failing him.

"Damn right, you shouldn't have come!" Lou retorted as Victoria shushed her away with her hand.

"He shouldn't have ever left, more like!" Victoria crossed her arms, standing in front of Colin, a furious glint in her eyes.

"Please," Charlotte begged, "please, stop this. We need to calm down."

"I'm sorry, but you all need to leave! I won't have these dramatics in my café; you're disturbing my regulars." The red-faced café owner stood before their table with his arms folded across his chest.

"She's just passed out!" Lou protested, "You can't just throw her out on the street!"

The others all murmured their agreement.

"Och, let 'em stay Donnie, this is the most entertainment we've seen since old Jock Dawson choked on his Eccles cake!" an elderly, jolly-looking man, who was clearly a regular customer, called out.

Guffaws of laughter rang out around the café and even Donnie had to smother a smirk.

The café owner looked sympathetically at Charlotte and sighed. "Ok, she can stay. I'll get her some water, but the rest of you... wait, I recognise you lot! Out! Except for her," he indicated Charlotte.

As he bustled the cat ladies to the door, with cries of "outrageous!" from Victoria and "do you know who I am?" from Lou, Colin sat down next to Charlotte.

"We need to talk," he said.

Chapter Thirty-Five

Lou

The five of them gathered together outside the café just as a burly Scot came jogging down the beach. "Oh no," Lou said a little too loudly. "Isn't that the bloke we almost ran down?"

He heard her and skidded to a halt in front of them. "Well, lassies, looks like you're up to no good again." He suddenly bent over and retrieved something out of the sand. "Well, well," he murmured and approached Lou. "I believe this belongs to ye!"

Lou stared at the broken heel from her shoe. "It does," she said, taking it from him, their fingers touching briefly, making her aware of an unexpected tingling as if this guy could become—well, more than a stranger. "I'm sorry we scared you," she began.

He roared with laughter and leaned over her. "Ye cannot scare me, little lass."

Lou, already tall, who intentionally wore high heels to make herself even taller, felt tiny next to this giant of a man. He made her feel feminine.

He strode onto the deck up to the café door and looked in. "So, it appears ye've found your other lassie's fellow. Colin, wasn't it?"

"Yes," Victoria answered angrily, irritating Lou who was sidling up to the Scot wondering how she might get to know him better. "Colin's a real creep!" Victoria added dryly.

Lizzie put her hand on Victoria's arm. "It's important to forgive people even if there's no chance of reconciliation," she whispered.

Lou sighed deeply, realis   ing Lizzie probably wanted Victoria to forgive *her* for taking up with a man.

Ruthie, with a whimsical look on her face, smiled slightly. "I'd take my husband back in a heartbeat if I could. I've been angry he deserted me by dying, leaving me with the B & B all by myself. You just never know what's coming," she said sadly.

Cathy nodded in agreement. "So true!"

"You can say that again," Lou muttered, stepping onto the deck and staring through a window into the café. "Oh my God!" she yelled, seeing Charlotte with arms around Colin who had his head resting on her shoulder, tears dripping onto her blouse. "God, Colin is crying. I wish the Second Chance Saloon crew were here to film this. Maybe we can stage it later when they get here!"

The Scot threw her a sidelong glance and opened the door but before he went inside, Lou yelled, "What's your name, Jock?"

His hand on the doorknob, he stopped. "Who wants to know?"

"How would you like to be on my show, Second Chance Saloon?"

He shrugged. "My wife watches that show so probably not."

Lou felt her shoulders sag. She hadn't noticed a wedding ring on his finger but that didn't mean much. What a fool she was: the last thing she wanted was to get involved with another married man.

Victoria approached her. Lou waited for the expected barb, but to her surprise Victoria sympathised, "It's so hard to find a soulmate or even a partner who will treat you with respect and be a decent companion."

"You deserve better," the Scot said kindly to both of them. "My name is Andrew MacGregor. Yours?" He looked down on Lou with a sparkle in his eyes.

Lou didn't intend to answer until he remarked through a chuckle. "Yep, we all deserve better. My wife, or I should say my ex-wife, is a cow and I don't want a second chance with her, thank you very much."

"Oh," Lou cried. "We'd match you with someone entirely different of course." She smiled.

"And your name is?"

"I'm Lou, the creator and director of Second Chance Saloon. I'm also an actress."

Victoria turned her head away to hide her smirk at Lou's untruthful self-title.

"I'd like to explore being in your show, Louise," Andrew said with a grin.

Victoria groaned. "That's good for you, Lou, because now that we've found Colin and reunited Charlotte with him, I am going to book a flight home. There are no second chances for me. I need a first chance."

Chapter Thirty-Six

Victoria

Once back in London, Victoria let herself into her front door, feeling more solitary than she'd ever felt in her life. As she shut the door behind her, she sighed in relief. *It's over,* she thought gratefully, then, with a twitch of her head, *Where's Biscuit?*

As if hearing her mum's thoughts, Biscuit appeared from the kitchen, rubbing her pretty orange head against the wall as she approached.

"Hello, my darling," Victoria cooed, bending down to pick up what felt like her only companion in the world right now.

"Ooh, did you miss me? I missed you!" Picking Biscuit up and planting a kiss on her wet nose, Victoria felt a sharp pang of emptiness and regret. She hugged the little fur ball close and took a deep breath, her decision made.

Placing the little ginger cat down, she stood and steadied her shoulders, and walked to the living room where she sank into the sofa, with a gulp of sorrow.

Sobs overwhelmed her: a lamentation of her grief, her sham of a marriage, her lost closeness with Lizzie, and her sheer loneliness. Biscuit jumped up onto her lap. "I'm okay, my darling," Victoria spoke through her cries, as the little orange feline licked her salty tears away. "I will be okay anyway," she sniffed.

Two days ago, she'd heard from Lou that Charlotte and Colin had taken themselves off for a deep talk, which apparently was more than fine with Lou, since she was going to dinner with Andrew MacGregor. Victoria had rolled her eyes at the thought of those two probably, knowing Lou, heading to bed. Now, she shook her head and sat down to write a letter.

It was time.

For too long, she had put this off.

But at least nobody knew, at least, she didn't think they did. She was just a young girl. Every time her uncle and aunt used to visit with their sons, her older cousins, Paul and James, they'd send them and her out into the garden to play.

And they did play, and Victoria didn't realise what those boys made her do was wrong. She was too young to understand much. It went on for four years and Victoria never said a word.

Until one summer when Victoria had just turned twelve. The very thought of her mother's response still made her shudder. Her mother commented on how fat her belly was getting. Then at long last Victoria opened her mouth and told the truth.

And then she got sent to the home, where she, being told what a dirty slut she was, had to fight the pain of pushing her child from her immature body. She was forced to give the little baby boy away, whilst her milky breasts were screaming for him, and her heart cracked into a thousand pieces.

As Biscuit stretched out on her lap, she shook her head. She had held her feelings back for too long: she should never have let this go on so long. "What do you think, my sweet?" she asked the cat, who reached up to touch her lips with her nose.

At least her cat still loved her. She smiled, tears pooling in her eyes. "Yes, you're right, it's time."

Dear son, she wrote, but before she composed another word, there was a rap on the door. She almost ignored it, but the rapping became more insistent. She gently put Biscuit down and laid the letter on the nearby table. "Alright, alright, I'm coming," she said crossly and slung open the door, more than a little surprised to see Lou grinning at her. "May I come in?" she asked.

"This is not a good time," Victoria remarked. "I'm busy."

Lou was not one to ever be put off. "Your eyes look red. Have you been crying? Let me make you a cup of tea."

Victoria reluctantly stepped aside for Lou to enter. She was about to direct Lou to the kitchen, but the woman stooped down and grabbed the letter off the table. "What the fuck!" She eyed Victoria. "You never told anyone you had a kid. My God, you have a son. What happened to him?"

"It's nobody's business but mine," Victoria retorted.

Lou looked her up and down and shook her head. "Is he still alive? she asked morosely and added hopefully, "How old is he?"

Victoria groaned as the words slipped from her clenched mouth. "He was born exactly forty-two years ago today. That was the last time I ever saw him."

"My God!" Lou's eyes widened. "You must have been a child yourself!" She put her hand over her eyes. "My God! I'm so sorry and it is none of my business, but just know you weren't to blame for whatever happened to you."

Victoria sank into a chair, trying not to cry, hating to show weakness, but it was no good, the floodgates opened, and she began to sob.

Lou comforted her the only way she knew how by fetching a bottle of gin from a nearby sideboard and digging out two glasses. She poured them both a double, into the long-stemmed martini glasses she'd put on the side table and wrapped her arms around Victoria who quickly shrugged her away and took a long slug of the gin. "This needs dry vermouth and an olive," she remarked wryly. "This has been a bad day for me, that's all." She hoped Lou would take the hint and not pursue the subject.

Lou sipped her drink thoughtfully. 'I came to ask you if you'd be on my show again. The footage in Scotland with Colin and Charlotte was a huge hit. It's on YouTube if you want to watch it and it's gone viral, so I'll have to have a follow-up show about them. Meanwhile, I'd love to find someone for you to love. Everyone deserves to have a decent relationship, you know."

"I am not interested!" Victoria stated firmly. "And anyway, you can hardly call the Scotland saga a hit. The only images of Charlotte and Colin on the video was their attempts to run away from your cameraman and your incessant meddling!"

"OO, ooo! I have a brilliant idea." Lou ignored her. "Why don't I contact your son, and you can both be on my show? After all, it is about second chances, right? People would love it!"

Victoria's mouth gaped open, and she had half a notion to throw the remainder of her gin into Lou's face, but instead she shook her head. "No way!" was all she could manage, and hoped Lou would respect her privacy.

"Suit yourself," Lou harrumphed. "Mind you, I say Colin and Charlotte's reunion was a success, but only in the sense that it ended in a bit of a cliffhanger. Charlotte basically told him she still wants him but needs to think. Victoria, are you listening?"

Victoria glared at Lou. "You just discovered my deepest, darkest secret, something I still haven't come to terms with myself, and here you are wittering on about your show? Is there no limit to your vanity?"

Lou's mouth fell open and Victoria slammed her gin glass on the table. "Please, just leave me in peace, Lou. I need today, I..." Victoria gulped back a sob, "I need to grieve."

Even Lou could tell when enough was enough. "Let me know if there's any way I can help." And with a pat of Victoria's shoulder, she took her leave.

Chapter Thirty-Seven

Charlotte

It seemed years ago when Charlotte last sat in her living room, like she was now, waiting for the cat ladies who'd become her friends and allies. Their insistence on taking her to Scotland where she'd found Colin after three years hadn't resolved the issue with him, but their support filled her with gratitude. They'd even supported her through her ex, John's surgery, including Lou making room for her daughter in her apartment.

Women friends were the very best. She loved their ability to put differences aside and help one another. Thinking about them made her chuckle at some of their conversations: Lou was flashy and outlandish, but beneath that veneer was a person who did care, if you dug deeply enough anyway.

Victoria was stern and aloof, but she did her best to organise and to help. Lizzie was kind but had a streak of determination and understanding about what really mattered, and Cathy was, well, she was helpful and gentle, if only she appreciated her own qualities. Charlotte wondered how she'd ever gotten on before these women came into her life.

During the debacle in Scotland, she'd hinted she wanted to get back with Colin, but in fact she was completely undecided. The man had been gone for three years living in Australia, working on the Great Barrier Reef, and there was no reason for him not to have contacted her. He'd explained that once in Australia, he'd had a sort of middle-age-crisis and had found himself wondering if what he had was enough. Was he settling? Was this all there was in life, when there was this great big world before him?

Charlotte had almost slapped his sorry face for that!

He'd asked her to forgive him, told her he never stopped loving her but, once time had passed, it had gotten harder to get back in touch with her.

He'd asked her to come up to Scotland to live with him in his new house. It was smaller than hers and pleasant enough, but she loved her house here and her furniture and her cat, Mirabelle, who currently sat on the arm of the couch, purring. Not to mention, it wouldn't be so easy to get another job teaching, especially not at the university level. He'd even had the nerve to suggest she could get an apartment in Edinburgh and teach at the university. Then, he'd said, they could spend weekends together. The man was delusional. And yet, she was tempted. Her kids would soon be going back home to America, and her ex, John, would be leaving even sooner, once the hospital had given him the all-clear to fly. So, exactly where was her home? Was there really anything to keep her here in London? Sure, she loved the culture but rarely went to the theatre, and only occasionally to the National Art Gallery above Trafalgar Square, let alone to poetry readings, or concerts etc.

The cat ladies thought Colin was after her money. But who knew? He wasn't without funds: he'd had enough to finally go through with the purchase of the house he now lived in, and he'd gotten a job with the Scottish Environmental Protection Agency. She didn't readily make friends and the thought of starting in a new place, even if welcomed, would not be easy. Although, she'd found a kindred spirit in Ruthie, so there was that.

"What shall I do, Mirabelle?" she murmured, winding a few strands of her cat's long fur around her fingers. Maybe having friends like the cat ladies would be enough to keep her here, she thought, as she waited for them to arrive. The wine was ready, the glasses sparkling, along with a tray of hors d'oeuvres on the table in her dining room. She'd bought sausage rolls, sushi, mini quiches, and baked fresh chocolate chip cookies. Hopefully, there was something for everyone.

After they were all comfortably seated, wine glasses in their hands, Charlotte opened the conversation beyond the usual polite hellos. "What's going on with you, Victoria? We really missed you driving on the way back from Inverness."

Lou didn't give her a chance to reply. "It was great that Mac came with us to help."

Victoria shook her head, and the others smiled half-heartedly.

"What?" Lou said. "He's great!"

Charlotte put her hand on Lou's knee in a kind gesture. "Don't rush into anything, Lou. You're on the rebound from that creep who strung you along for years."

"I know," she said, "but Mac is different. He's kind and considerate and wants to be with me."

Victoria stared at her shoes, and they were all quiet until she stammered. "He might have secrets, Lou. Perhaps unthinkable things from his past."

All of them looked at Victoria, waiting for more, but she'd turned bright red and was gulping back her wine.

Cathy clapped her hands. "I love secrets. Let's all share one!"

"No!" Lou cried, glancing sideways at Victoria.

"It's okay, Lou," Victoria said. "I am ready to reveal my truth. I just ask for you all to keep matters to yourselves."

By the time Victoria finished telling them about giving birth all alone as a thirteen-year-old child, they were all crying.

"We'll help you find your son," Lizzie said, between sobs.

"Of course we will," remarked Cathy, wiping her eyes.

Lizzie stared momentarily into space. "You've suffered, Victoria, and it wasn't your fault. Men need to be held to account too. So, who was the father?"

Victoria looked mortified. "It won't help to know. Immediately after I was sent to the home for single mothers, their parents moved them to Australia."

"This must be so painful for you, Victoria," Cathy said thoughtfully.

"It is. But I want to at least know my son's name and that he's okay!"

"We're good at finding missing men." Lou arched her well-plucked eyebrows. "We can help you locate him, and maybe the father too, who we probably ought to thrash."

Victoria grimaced. "I have no idea even where to begin."

"Don't worry, Doll. We've got your back!"

Charlotte wondered what they'd set in motion.

Chapter Thirty-Eight

Lizzie

Lizzie's heart felt heavy as Victoria told her heartbreaking story. Why had she never mentioned her son before? Okay, Lizzie accepted they weren't as close now as they used to be, but they once were almost inseparable. Hellfire, she'd even, almost, considered an intimate relationship with her! But for Victoria to withhold such a sad secret past almost offended her.

Glancing at Victoria now, her face stained with spent tears, Lizzie felt suddenly ashamed of her selfish thoughts. "We will help you find your son, Victoria." She reached out and clutched Victoria's hand, looking around at the other cat ladies as they nodded their heads in agreement.

Victoria smiled sadly, sniffing as she tried to compose herself. Typical Victoria, Lizzie thought, not unkindly, always a stiff upper lip in the face of adversity.

"Thank you, ladies," Victoria squeezed Lizzie's hand before standing and smoothing the pleats of her beige skirt. "I must use the loo."

As she glided out of Charlotte's living room, the remaining cat ladies looked at each other, mouths wide open.

"Well," said Charlotte, "I think that calls for something stronger than wine."

"Tequila!" Lou shouted and Cathy groaned whilst Charlotte giggled, "We're not in Ibiza, Lou!"

Lizzie smiled, watching her friends with their banter. She really was fond of them, she thought.

"How about some of that fine Scotch Whiskey I brought back from our little, erm, trip?" Charlotte suggested.

"Speaking of our 'trip'," Victoria said, walking back into the room, gesturing quotation marks with her fingers, "what's going on with you and Colin?"

Charlotte visibly sagged, and placing the whiskey bottle onto the coffee table, she sank back into her seat. "Where to start…" she murmured.

"The beginning is usually good," Lou quipped, sitting forward to pour the amber liquid into her empty wine glass.

"He wants me to move there, to Scotland." Charlotte sighed.

"What?" Victoria looked outraged. "After all that man put you through, I hope you're not considering it!"

Charlotte remained silent as the ladies gawped at her.

"Charlotte, you're not, are you?" Lizzie asked quietly, studying Charlotte's lovely face.

"I don't know," she finally admitted.

"Ridiculous!" Victoria slammed her drink down, the coffee table shuddering under the thud, glasses tinkling.

"Good on ya, queen!" Lou exclaimed, "everyone deserves a second chance."

Victoria shook her head, a look of pure disdain on her face as she looked from Lou to Charlotte. "You're a fool," she declared.

Lizzie hurriedly intervened, hoping to defuse the tension that was making everyone twitchy. "I really think it's up to Charlotte," she said pointedly to Victoria, albeit in a gentle tone. Ignoring Victoria's glare, Lizzie continued, "what are you thinking, Charlotte?"

Charlotte pursed her lips, searching for the right words.

"Maybe there's nothing for me here anymore, maybe a fresh start in a new place wouldn't be such a bad thing."

"Excuse me?" Lou stood up, animated as ever. "Nothing here for you? What about us, your friends? I mean…" She was suddenly quiet, and Lizzie thought she'd never seen Lou more unsure of herself than right now. "I mean, we are friends, aren't we?"

Even the usually no-nonsense Victoria had tears in her eyes as she watched the lively Lou, now almost childlike, gaze down at the floor.

"Of course we are!" Charlotte spurted, "I just…"

"I think," Victoria interrupted, "I think we're all just starting to realise how much we need each other." Little red spots suddenly bloomed on her cheeks, as she spoke with the closest to affection she'd ever displayed.

"We really are. I'll be honest, initially, this book club thing was just an excuse to get out of the house," Lizzie confessed shyly. "But now, it's, *you're,* so much more than that."

Charlotte wiped a tear and smiled.

"You're so right. In fact, I have all the time in the world to decide about Colin. After all," she picked up the whiskey bottle, "he made *me* wait three years!" With that, she put the bottle to her lips and slugged it back.

"Amen to that!" Lou whooped and the other ladies howled and cheered, causing poor little Mirabelle to scarper from the corner of the room where she'd been sleeping.

"But for now, we need a plan." Lizzie declared and looked around at the puzzled faces.

Lizzie settled her gaze on Victoria. "We're going to find your boy, Victoria."

Victoria smiled and nodded graciously.

"Hell yes!" Lou snatched the bottle from Charlotte and swigged, loudly gulping back the Scotch as the ladies all laughed.

"Now," said Lizzie, once she'd composed herself. "Where do we start?"

And so the discussions began...

Chapter Thirty-Nine

Cathy

Cathy took a few moments while the others were slugging back whiskey. "I have a secret to tell," she remarked.

Lou angrily slammed her glass on the table. Lizzie's lips thinned in disgust. Charlotte's eyes narrowed, puzzled. And Victoria appeared as if she might throw up. "Dear God," she muttered.

"No, no, no, not that," Cathy dismissively waved her hands in the air. "It's nothing so ugly as what happened to Victoria. It's not ugly at all!"

"What the fuck?" Lizzie asked, slurring a little.

"I talk to my cat," Cathy responded.

"Now that's crazy." Lizzie giggled.

"The question is does the cat talk back?" Charlotte intervened with a smile.

"Not exactly," Cathy began, but was interrupted by Victoria snatching away her wine glass. "I think you've had one too many!"

"No," Cathy retorted. "I haven't even touched the whiskey! Molly *does* talk to me but not how you mean. She always meows hello in the morning and blinks her eyes at me to tell me she loves me, and she also licks her lips to let me know when she's hungry. But whenever I've had a perplexing problem, she sits on my lap, and I stroke her soft fur, and muse. Then all of sudden, an idea will pop into my mind that is the answer I need."

"For God's sake!" scoffed Victoria, secretly thinking of her many one-way conversations with Biscuit.

Lizzie shook her head but wasn't quite as disbelieving. "It sounds almost prayerful."

Lou started to laugh. "I guess I should stick to cats as my number ones," she quipped. "Or maybe I'll become a vicar!"

"Be careful what you wish for." Charlotte frowned. "Seriously now, let's get back to Victoria." She smiled gently at Victoria. "What can you remember from that time? We know your son's date of birth. Do you remember the name of the unwed mother's home where you were sent?"

"And what's the name of the creep who did this to you?"

Victoria covered her face with her hands before grabbing the bottle of whiskey and draining it. "It wasn't a boy. It was boys!" She moaned.

And after a stunned silence, added. "They were my cousins. One held me down, and the other, well you know…And I froze! They said if I told anyone, they'd beat me up."

Cathy gasped. "That's dreadful! You poor thing. Was your baby premature?"

"I don't think so," Victoria responded. "I didn't know anything about sex or carrying a child, but I remember one of the nuns telling me the baby was a good size and seemed healthy."

"Thank God," Cathy continued. "Children born to parents who are related can have genetic issues…"

Lou held up her hand. "Stop!" she ordered. "Let's find Victoria's son! He's probably fine!"

Charlotte was pensive. "If you find him, it might be better to wait a while before you contact him, Victoria. He may not know he's been adopted and if he does, who knows what he was told about his birth parents."

"He needs to know," Cathy said quietly. "He might have heart problems or immunity issues that can be treated to prevent future issues."

"And those boys need to be found and held accountable. For all we know they are serial rapists!"

"Jesus!" Lizzie stared at the ceiling.

Victoria groaned. "I won't *ever* be the one to tell my son he is a child of rape and incest!"

Chapter Forty

Victoria

The 'Our Lady of Hearts' building looked big, imposing and cold and even after all these years, it made Victoria shudder. She suddenly wanted to weep, reduced to her thirteen-year-old self, begging her mother not to leave her, literally clinging to her waist as her mother extracted herself. As a young and confused Victoria looked to the only adult she knew and trusted, her mother said the oft repeated words, "Dirty slut!"

She entered the reception area in a daze, memories flooding her mind: *"I'm sorry, Mummy," she cried, but without any idea as to why she was there, what she had done wrong. "Don't leave me, Mum!" she wailed to her mother's retreating back, but her mother hustled away, shouting over her shoulder, "I'll be back to collect you once you've delivered the devil's spawn."*

Victoria jumped when a hand on her back startled her.

"Hey, it's just me," Lizzie whispered. "You okay?"

Victoria nodded, swallowing the lump in her throat and thrusting aside the painful memory of her mother's betrayal.

"You don't have to do this if you're not ready," Charlotte interjected.

"I'm ready," Victoria uttered as the nun appeared behind the desk.

"Bless you, ladies, how may I help?" The gracious elderly lady with kind brown eyes smiled at the assembled group. "I'm Sister Estavious." Her wide beamed smile couldn't help but elicit smiles from the ladies.

Victoria stepped forward cautiously. "I…" she faltered, unable to continue.

"She had a son here, forty-two years ago, when this bullshit was allowed, and nobody investigated sexual abuse!"

Lou, of course. She stepped between Victoria and the elderly nun who, surprisingly, didn't appear particularly shocked.

"We were not an illegal baby trade, but we did help out young mothers…" the nun began.

"Helped?" Victoria found her voice. "I was thirteen years old when that baby was ripped from my body. Not once was I asked if I wanted him, nor was I asked how he got there!"

The elderly nun closed her eyes and nodded, "Yes, times were different back then." She quickly waved away Lou's potential interruption and continued, "They really were different, and Doctor Peterson tried her best but…"

Victoria was almost breathless. "I remember a kind lady doctor who examined me. She was young and pretty. I was so embarrassed, but she reassured me. Is she still here?"

The elderly nun shook her head, looking suddenly wary. "I'm not allowed to give out privileged information. Doctor Peterson left soon after you…"

"Amelia Peterson?" Lou shouted. "She's a plastic surgeon now!"

The elderly nun sighed and shuffled some papers on the desk. "There's nothing more I can add. I'm sorry. Let me show you out."

"Well, many thanks, Sister Malarkey," Lou cried. "Let's go get the car. I know her, this Amelia; she did my Botox and fillers back in 2005!"

"That's why you look so good?" Charlotte murmured and followed the nun and Lou out of the door.

Victoria was numb as they went outside. She took a backward glance at the place where she'd lost her childhood. No, wrong, she'd lost her childhood long before she went there.

Here was where she'd lost her child. Suddenly, with a steely determination, she felt strong and brave.

"Go, Lou! For once your vanity has benefited one of us. Let's go find that bloody doctor!"

"You got it, Doll!" Lou put her foot down and screeched out of the driveway as Sister Estavious, still standing in the doorway, crossed herself and shook her head, a bemused frown on her wizened face.

Chapter Forty-One

Charlotte

As Lou gunned the car racing for the doctor's office where she'd gone for her Botox treatments, Lizzie was hanging on to the side of the door, Cathy looked stricken, Victoria seemed exhausted, and only, she, Charlotte had her senses about her. "Cats," she said quietly. "This is probably a wild goose chase. Sorry, Lou, but I cannot imagine why a plastic surgeon would have been delivering unwanted babies over forty years ago. She'd be, what, in her seventies now?"

Lou's shoulders sagged and she slowed down. "Oh, I just wanted to help!"

"I know," Victoria said. "Cathy, you're a nurse. What do you think?"

"It's really difficult to trace a baby that's been given up for adoption, and I doubt even if this doctor delivered babies she'd have any records of where the child was placed." Cathy reached forward and laid her hand on Victoria's shoulder. "But since we are almost at the medical centre, let's see if Dr. Peterson can tell us anything, maybe guide us in some way."

Lou parked and led the way, stopping briefly at reception to ask to see the doctor, but was told she was with another patient.

"This is an emergency," Lou cried, and the receptionist immediately called through to the examining rooms. A nurse ushered Lou and the others, like a bunch of kittens, scurrying past reception to the treatment rooms. They were crowded together in the tiny space next to an examining table with stirrups that made them all squirm.

"What's going on, Lou? the nurse asked.

Charlotte felt such a fraud, but Lou was a better actress than she'd ever given her credit for. She pushed her hand against her forehead. "I only want to tell the doctor," She whispered.

Within five minutes, a white-coated lady physician came in. She looked around at the others.

"We're her support group," Charlotte said.

The doctor nodded and addressed Lou who spat out her hopes that she was the doctor who'd delivered Victoria's baby.

Dr. Peterson groaned. "Ladies," she said. "I am not an Ob Gyn and have never delivered babies. Furthermore, when your child was born over forty years ago, I was still in nappies. I doubt any doctor will be able to assist you from so long ago. I certainly cannot help you. Go back to the home and see if they keep records. Otherwise, you might try local agencies that keep birth records. Perhaps, the church associated with the facility where you were taken will open up their files to you." She patted Victoria's arm. "I am so sorry for what you went through. Hopefully, that particular facility will be able to help you more." She moved briskly towards the door. "Good luck!" And she was gone.

Back in the car, Charlotte started the conversation. "Let's go online to see if there are any groups who reunite long parted mothers and kids, sisters with sisters, and so on. You read about it all the time, right? And I'm pretty sure the nuns are never going to admit to having the records, even if they do."

"I don't want my name on the Internet," Victoria moaned.

"I don't blame you. But we can anonymously plug in the birthdate and the home and see if anything comes up. I'll do it on my computer for you, if you like," Charlotte offered.

"Or," Lou added, starting up the car and pulling out into the main road. "Or we break into the "home" tonight and check out their files ourselves."

"Not a good idea," Charlotte replied, rolling her eyes. "We don't need another arrest on our records. Let's look on the Internet first to see if there's any info about Our Lady of Hearts."

Chapter Forty-Two

Lou

"Hello, darling boy!" Lou reached down to pet Peregrine, her handsome Manx cat. She'd just got home from the set and was ready to crash on the sofa with a glass of wine, but her mobile began to ring.

Searching through her bag, Lou grabbed the phone and answered without checking the caller ID. "Changed your mind about the break-in plan?" She laughed into the phone.

"Erm, excuse me? Lou?"

With a rush of realisation at the deep Scottish tones at the end of the line, Lou's hands flew to her chest and a dark crimson blush consumed her. He'd gone back to Scotland after only two days in London where he'd been a gentleman and insisted upon staying in a hotel. She'd longed for him to stay with her. He wasn't like any of the men she usually hooked up with, who were more than willing to hop into bed with her. She felt rejected when Andrew 'Mac' MacGregor wouldn't oblige. What was wrong with him? But that voice! "Andrew? Gosh, what must you think? That break-in comment, it's an inside joke!"

His soft low chuckle relieved her panic. "Well, I certainly hope so," he laughed, "or that would be a whole different kind of tv show!"

Lou burst into dainty giggles. "It most certainly would!" she agreed. "So, to what do I owe the pleasure?"

"Well, here's the thing," Mac began tentatively, "I happen to find myself in London, I'm hungry and I could really use a dinner companion."

"Oh," Lou was hesitant for a whole second, "You want me to go for dinner with you?"

"Well, break-in's allowing, yes. If you're free?" Lou could hear Mac holding his breath at the end of the line.

"Now, let me see," she decided to keep him hanging a while longer. After all, treat 'em mean, keep 'em keen! "I'll have to rearrange a few things," Lou began, glancing around her living room and thinking all she had to rearrange were the scatter cushions on her sofa, but he wasn't to know that.

"Forgive me," Mac interrupted, "I'm being presumptuous. I've no right to assume you'll just drop everything to meet me for dinner. Sorry, I..."

"No! No! It's fine, of course it's fine!" Lou almost squealed down the phone, panicked that keeping him hanging had been a bad idea.

"It is?" Lou could hear the smile in his voice.

"It is," she smiled too. "Now where shall I meet you?"

Dashing into her bedroom after arranging to meet Mac at Charing Cross station, Lou flung open her vast wardrobe. *What to wear, what to wear!* She flustered as she whipped through rack after rack of dresses, finally settling on her favourite little black number, with sequins around the sweetheart neckline. That and a pair of killer heels would do the job nicely, she mused as she flung it on the bed and settled herself in front of the mirror at her dressing table. This time, he wouldn't be able to resist.

Rifling through her expensive make up bag, searching for her brightest crimson lipstick, she heard her mobile ringing again. *Please don't cancel!* she pleaded silently as she flew back into the lounge to answer the call.

With a puzzled expression she saw it was Victoria calling. A rarity in itself, not least because despite the recent bonding of the cat ladies, Lou knew she was Victoria's least favourite of them. "Hi Doll, how you doing?" She answered the call, looking at the clock on the mantelpiece, mindful of the lack of time she had to get ready.

"Lou..."

Lou could barely make out the words through the sobbing at the end of the line. "What is it? What's happened?" Lou felt the anxiety and fear spike her heart. Had something happened to one of the cat ladies?

"It's..." Victoria was struggling to speak, and Lou pushed her.

"Victoria, please, what's wrong?"

"I just can't... I suddenly..."

"Suddenly what?" Lou was getting impatient now, yet at the same time, she knew that for stoic and practical Victoria to be in such a state of despair this, whatever it was, was bad.

"I remembered something..." Victoria sniffed down the phone.

"About your baby? About the boys who raped you? Weren't they your cousins?"

Victoria sobbed harder and Lou rolled her eyes, knowing she was being unkind, but come on!

"Yes, about my son, I remembered that..."

Lou steeled herself, again checking the clock and figuring she was going to be late anyway. "Tell me, Doll," she said, more gently now, "what did you remember?"

Chapter Forty-Three

Victoria

Two days later, while Victoria waited for the other cat ladies to arrive, she cuddled Biscuit, memories flooding her. She hoped no one would notice her red swollen eyes from crying. It was bad enough she'd called Lou of all people for a shoulder to cry on. She didn't even like the woman that much, but she had to admit, Lou was a good friend when you were in a dark hole you couldn't climb out of on your own. Lou had even been willing to cancel her dinner with that Scot, but Victoria had insisted she needed to go, even though she had her doubts about his motives. But that went with the territory for her after the horrible betrayal she had experienced as a child. And it wasn't just giving birth when she was completely ill-prepared and way too young, it was her mother's and her father's inability to protect her, followed by their scorn and coldness towards her after she'd got back from the Home.

Not only had they forced her to give up her baby, but she'd also lost her beloved Big Teddy, a stuffed bear given to her by her aunt, the one whose boys had treated her unspeakably. Not that any of them even realised the grief she'd been experiencing and was still experiencing, wondering what had happened to her baby, and remembering Big Teddy with his ragged ears and flat black nose.

The only time she'd seen her baby was when another girl at the home, who was a little older, led her to the nursery in the middle of the night and pointed out her infant who was in a cradle in the middle of several other infants. The glimpse of the sweet baby filled her with love, and she knew he would have loved her too. She'd felt a strong urge to pick him up but didn't dare. She'd wanted to do something for him, but she had no power. She did have Big Teddy, though, clutched against her chest. She gently laid him next to the baby, hoping he'd be allowed to keep him, and it would comfort him and let him know she loved him and would never let any harm come to him.

She was hopeful, yet at the same time, she dreaded what Charlotte, who said she had some information, might have found on the Internet. Victoria's heart pounded when there was a rap on the door. Biscuit leaped down and hid under an end table while she wiped her eyes, doing her best to appear composed.

Lizzie and Cathy were together, followed shortly by Charlotte and finally, Lou. Victoria had nothing ready for them, but Lizzie made them tea and brought in two pots, kept hot in cozies along with five mugs and a strainer on a tray. And she'd found a tin of biscuits to offer them.

While they nibbled and sipped without saying much of anything, Lou dug in her oversized bag and pulled out a tissue-wrapped package and handed it to Victoria. "To comfort you at night," she murmured.

Victoria sat her cup on the side table and ripped away the tissue. She held out a soft cuddly bear and began to cry.

Lou looked mortified. "I only meant to help. I'm sorry, V."

"Oh no, he's beautiful. It just hurts to remember Big Teddy who's probably in tatters by now, even if my baby got to keep him." The others waited to learn more, and Victoria obliged, adding, "This bear is sweet. I'll call him Teddy-Boy. There's only one thing missing." She unclasped the bracelet she was wearing and put it around the stuffed toy's leg. "There," she said. "That's better. Big Teddy was wearing a bracelet too, one I'd found at the Home. It was some sort of foreign coin that had been pierced and threaded with a blue ribbon." She stroked the coin on the bear's leg. "I always wore this one in memory."

Charlotte flipped open her laptop and tapped in a few keys to a website "You know," she said, "your bear might still be around. We can check on Antiques Roadshow or eBay. People are always trying to sell vintage bears. Anyway, almost certainly, the bracelet is intact, and it could be an identifying feature. But let's start at the beginning by following the directions on Find My Family Adoption Search and Reunion Registry. Okay?"

Chapter Forty-Four

Charlotte

Charlotte, with a desperate sense of longing to reunite Victoria with her son, frantically scrolled through the internet, but the adoption search website had, so far, yielded no results.

She couldn't begin to imagine what Victoria had been through. Such a young girl, abused and then forced to give up the result of such abuse, and so callously. It was no wonder she had become the cool, hardened lady that she was today. Although, there was a softness to Victoria now, a vulnerability that endeared her to the other cat ladies.

"Here!" The other cat ladies jumped as Charlotte screeched. "There's an item on eBay, a bracelet identical to the one you described, Victoria." Victoria looked wide-eyed at Charlotte and waited for her to continue.

"That's weird…" Charlotte mused, wrinkling her face as the others held their breath.

"What?" Lou implored, "tell us, Doll!"

"There's no price, the seller has simply left a note on the item." Charlotte glanced at Victoria who suddenly held her hand to her mouth.

Charlotte continued gazing into her laptop screen, then her mouth dropped wide open, tears filled her eyes, and she looked at Victoria.

"I think you'd better read this," she said softly, turning her laptop to Victoria.

This bracelet is not for sale; however, I thought this might be my only chance to find the previous owner. My brother was adopted by my parents before I was born. They had thought they couldn't conceive, so when they had the chance to adopt a son, forty-two years ago, they were delighted. Their joy was intensified when I arrived as a surprise conception, two years later, and we became a wonderful family of four.

We had a wonderful childhood, my brother and I: our parents doted on us and could not do enough for us. And this has continued, until now.

My brother has been diagnosed with a rare genetic condition which means he is in urgent need of a kidney. And that, sadly, is where our parents cannot help. I'm reaching out in the hope that somebody out there will spot this unusual bracelet with a (I think) Japanese coin attached and recognise it as that which was left with my newborn brother all those years ago.

If this helps, in any way, to find my brother's biological family, and to maybe save his life, it's all I can ask for. We are desperate as a family, not just myself and my elderly parents, but my brother's wife and two daughters: my young nieces. Please, if you recognise this bracelet, contact the seller on...

Everyone sat quietly in shock, unable to say one word of comfort or hope.

Lou wiped a lone tear from her heavily made-up face.

Cathy's face seemed pinched as if her heart might break at any moment.

Lizzie immediately rushed to Victoria's side, held her tightly, and let her sob into her shoulder.

Charlotte, though astonished at this latest turn of events, could at least see there was a positive here. If this was Victoria's son, there was a chance that not only could they be reunited, but she could save his life. Victoria could give her boy life, for the second time. She took a deep breath and spoke bravely, "Victoria, you need to reply."

Chapter Forty-Five

Lizzie

Lizzie cancelled her plans to have dinner with Bill. She suspected he was getting serious about her and, even though she was sure Bill was a gentle and kind bloke, the thought of her ex and his brutality made her shudder. Bill was funny, kind, and considerate, but she wanted to take things at her pace. He'd make a good life-partner, but she was yet unsure she ever wanted to be hitched to another man, no matter how thoughtful and nice he seemed.

Her thoughts switched to Victoria who was the main reason she'd cancelled the dinner. Victoria's issues far overshadowed Lizzie's. Lizzie'd called her friend every day since they'd found out about her son, and Victoria had told her she had not responded to the email about him. She couldn't! She just couldn't! She'd also said she didn't want any company, but Lizzie knew she was fretting and worrying and probably drinking gallons of gin.

Come to think of it, all of the cat ladies seemed trapped in having to make life-changing decisions. Charlotte had yet to decide about continuing life with Colin or not. In fact, she'd called her once-missing husband in Scotland, and when a woman answered she'd almost flown off the handle. The woman, it turned out, was a friend of Ruthie's who was going over to clean Colin's house once a week. Speaking of Ruthie: she too was in the middle of decision making about whether or not to keep the B & B. And Lou, as impulsive as she could be, was in a conundrum about Andrew MacGregor who'd come to London and tried to persuade her to return to Inverness with him. Lizzie half-smiled remembering Lou's shock that the man hadn't immediately jumped into bed with her. Not everyone was a sex-maniac, she thought wryly. Even Cathy, who seemed the most settled, was thinking about seeking a job as a nurse but didn't know if she'd have the stamina to be able to work again; full-time or even part-time.

"Jeez," Lizzie muttered to Tom who was on her lap, purring his head off. "Sorry boy," she said, giving him a cuddle before putting him down. "I have to go out to check on Victoria. I won't be long." The cat wandered away and settled in his bed, tucking his head between his paws.

Lizzie's intention of only staying a few minutes at Victoria's and having a cup of tea ended up with her becoming Victoria's confidante in ways they'd once shared. "Victoria," Lizzie told her, "You do not have to respond to the sister. Even if he is your son and your kidney is a match, it does not mean you have to give him one…"

"You don't get it, Lizzie!" Victoria wailed. "I let him down."

"You were a child! And what about the father or fathers?"

Victoria covered her eyes with her hands and groaned. "Maybe I got what I asked for," she muttered.

Lizzie's thoughts flashed to her ex and his brutality. "Of course you didn't," she cried. 'What happened to you was not your fault!"

"I don't know," Victoria said, taking a tissue from a nearby box on the kitchen table to wipe her eyes.

"You know, I was a grown woman, but even when my ex demanded sex from me and took what he wanted, I felt as if I was to blame for not being interested. *You* were a child. If anyone holds responsibility, it's your parents. Your mother and father ought to have been checking on you! And they were cruel to you too after you had the baby when they should have comforted you."

"I know," Victoria said. "But how am I to get in touch with my son and have to reveal to him just who his father was, not that I even know which of those bullies it was." Her eyes narrowed and her mouth drooped. "I googled potential birth defects of children from incestuous relationships! They were my first cousins!"

Lizzie realised there was no way she could convince Victoria she had not been to blame for what happened nor was she to blame for her son's illness. "What's important," she said, "is for you to decide how you want to proceed. As I said before, you are under no obligation to reveal that you are his mother. Since he's only forty-two, he'll be eligible for a kidney transplant and is probably already on the list."

"What if he's not? What if he dies and I miss my chance to meet him?"

"If you like, I can answer the email and ask for more details. I can pretend I know of you, and I can even say you're dead."

"Oh nooo!" Victoria shook her head. "I've already lived too much of a lie!"

Chapter Forty-Six

Cathy

Cathy wished she could end the stalemate for all of the cat ladies. She was sick of all their angst. She had enough of her own troubles, too, especially financial. After a night of too many wines, she began by replying anonymously to the eBay message from Victoria's son's adoptive sister, letting her know that she knew his mother.

Once that ball was in motion, she'd wanted to focus on Charlotte, to send a text to Colin from an unknown number, telling him that Charlotte was moving on without him, and he shouldn't get in touch again, apart from any correspondence via their divorce lawyers. Except she did not have Colin's number.

She wanted to contact Lizzie's Bill, and inform him, anonymously of course, that Lizzie was not ready for anything serious, and he should give her some space.

Finally, Lou: she would love to inform that overbearing cad, Andrew MacGregor, that Lou was still hung up on her ex married lover, and he should, therefore, give up on his wooing of her. She didn't have his number or address either.

And now, Cathy sat back in her armchair, her cat, Molly, the beautiful, yet aging, blue grey feline, on her lap, musing about how to proceed. The email had been easy to send. It should do the trick of reuniting Victoria with her son and potentially giving him a kidney.

She smiled and stroked her furry friend. "It will all be for the best, my darling," she sighed wistfully.

Molly purred, overjoyed at being her mistress's centre of attention.

"I'm a nurse," Cathy continued, "I am supposed to make people feel better and I wish I could feel better too. What about me? Don't I deserve a break?" She'd applied to four hospitals, and none had shown any sign of wanting to hire her. She felt like an invisible old hag with nothing left to offer.

Sensing her owner's anger, Molly pricked back her ears, ready to pounce off her lap.

"And I am being kind," Cathy continued, "because I want to free them from the burdens they carry!"

Cathy clenched her fists and Molly jumped off, scurrying into the hallway. Cathy got up and went over to the fireplace. Her image in the mirror above the fireplace made her feel even more wretched: spittle pooled in the creases of her mouth reminding her she had forgotten to take her pain meds; not that she needed them except they did help her to feel better. But she was not about to become an addict.

When the doorbell rang, Cathy quickly puffed up her hair, and ran into the hallway to the front door.

"Hello, Cathy," Lou announced herself, "I think it's time we talk..."

"Of course." Cathy smiled whilst her heart raced. "Tea?" She stood aside to allow Lou to enter the hallway.

"I rather think this conversation may require something stronger, don't you think?" Lou gazed into Cathy's eyes, lips pursed, hands on her hips.

It felt as if the game was up, that Lou knew Cathy had tried to intervene, except she hadn't contacted that red-bearded Scot. Maybe now was the time to get his number and his address. "Take a seat, I'll get us some wine," Cathy gestured the living room and Lou plopped herself on the threadbare soda.

"Won't be a minute," Cathy sung as she entered her tiny kitchen, and grabbed a half empty bottle of red and filled two glasses. In the lounge, she handed one to Lou. "How's it going with Mac? And where did you say he lived exactly?" she asked disingenuously as if she was making small talk.

Lou frowned. "I'm not here to discuss Mac." She took a long gulp of her wine. "I want you, no need you, to appear on my show. The directors expect a production in two days, and I thought you'd be a perfect candidate. In fact, now you've mentioned Mac, he could be your unexpected partner." Lou chuckled. "He's in London now, that would teach him for turning down my offer of hospitality at my apartment."

Cathy sat there stunned at this unexpected turn of events. "You've got to be kidding. I don't want a man! Ever again."

"You only have to pretend to show interest." Lou smiled persuasively. "It would be fun, that's all!"

Seeing Cathy's pale face, Lou reached across and patted her knee gently.

"I'm joking, Doll! I mean, I do want you on my show, I'm desperate! No offence." Lou smiled, her bright red lips reminiscent of The Joker, in Cathy's eyes.

"And Mac?" Cathy asked.

Lou tutted and shook her head sadly. "No, I won't be having him on the show, I don't even know if he wants to be in my life."

This time, Cathy patted Lou's knee and was suddenly relieved she hadn't intervened in that particular problem.

Chapter Forty-Seven

Victoria

Victoria, paying no attention to the other women, stared at the small screen on her phone. She rarely used it for the Internet, but she wanted to re-read the notice from the adoptive sister. She didn't even know what this boy's, or man's rather, name was and the fact he had the foreign coin she'd left with her baby didn't really mean it was her son. Someone else might have taken the coin. She wished the print was bigger and brighter for her to decipher, but what she managed to read as she mulled over whether or not to offer her kidney came to nothing.

After the sister's initial notice there was an addendum:

Thank you to all who have wanted to help my brother. He continues to be in critical condition in the ICU. We are heartbroken that so many who responded were simply trying to get attention. Some even pretended to be the mother but upon following up, they had no real connection or worse they wanted money. And one woman even purported to know the mother, but she didn't bother to give her name, and without giving any helpful details only mentioned she lived in North London. Thus, I am taking this notice down tomorrow because it is too stressful to have our hopes raised and dashed repeatedly.

Victoria slumped in her chair and a tear rolled down her cheek.

The other cat ladies were chatting and drinking their wine while they listened to Haydn piano music that Charlotte thought they'd enjoy, but Lizzie intuitively glanced over. "Victoria," she cried. "Oh my God!"

They all looked up.

"Did he die?" Cathy asked with a deep sigh.

"No! I don't want to talk about it!" Victoria crossed her arms over her chest and managed to regain her composure. 'So, Cathy, are you really going to go on Second Chances?" Clearly she didn't care one way or the other, but Cathy's reply seemed a little off.

"No." She smiled sheepishly at Lou, "even though Lou threatened to bring Mac on. Although I'd like to speak to him, to make sure Lou isn't being taken for a fool by another man."

"I was joking about that!" Lou insisted. "Anyway, my relationship with Mac is none of your business, Cathy. And it's not your place to protect me," Lou said huffily.

"I'm a nurse and we help people not only physically, but also to make decisions they have trouble making."

"Such as?" Charlotte looked puzzled.

"Often patients' families can't come to terms with letting go of their terminally ill family members. One of the things I was able to do as an ICU nurse was help them see when a person clearly had no quality of life left. It is heartbreaking, but sometimes it's better to let people go."

"That's a bit different to relationship decisions!" Lizzie interjected.

Cathy ignored her and continued, "Charlotte, you ought to divorce Colin and get on with your own life. If it's too painful for you, I can send him a letter to tell him you're hiring divorce attorneys."

Charlotte looked taken aback by this outburst but nodded thoughtfully. "This isn't a life and death situation. I've made a good life here in Ickenham, but I've missed Colin, and I'm lonely."

"But can you forgive him?" Lizzie asked.

Victoria grabbed a tissue and blew her nose. "If my son dies, I won't be able to forgive myself. But how am I going to prove I'm the mother? Without having to also reveal the horrible way he was conceived?"

"We could check hospital ICUs for desperately ill kidney patients," Charlotte said. "Although, I once contacted every hospital I could think of about Colin, and despite me being his wife, no one would give me any information except to say he wasn't there."

Lou drummed her long fingernails up and down on the glass-topped table. "Cathy, why don't you see what you can find out? Don't you still have contacts from your hospital days?"

"Well, I have been trying to get hired by a hospital, so maybe I could pay the ones where I've applied a visit." She looked dubiously at Lou. "It's unlikely they'll tell me anything though."

"I could see if Bill, a lawyer, has any ideas where we stand from a legal perspective," Lizzie said as she blushed, "we've gotten pretty close."

Cathy frowned. "After what you've been through, it's too soon for you to rush into another romance!"

"Since when have you become our keeper, Cathy?" Lou muttered and then her eyes grew wide with new awareness. "It was you, wasn't it?"

"Me what?" Cathy stuttered.

"You sent that anonymous note to the sister about knowing who the mother was! You know, mentioning that she lived in North London!"

Cathy's bright red face gave her away. "I only meant to help!"

Victoria's shoulders got as stiff as a board. "I've a good mind to slap you!" But then she turned on her phone and began typing.

"Are you doing what I think you're doing?" Charlotte asked.

"Yes. I am trying to contact the sister before she deletes the notice. I'll tell her I'm from North London." She glared pointedly at Cathy. "Ickenham to be precise. And I won't be anonymous," She wailed. "But I don't know what to say exactly!"

Charlotte intervened. "Tell her the date you gave birth in Our Lady of Hearts and how young you were. Tell her about the teddy bear and the coin. Mention how you wish you'd been able to keep your baby but had no choice."

Victoria looked stricken.

"Be sure to give her your phone number. And keep your phone charged and turned on!" Lou told her.

Victoria, her eyes squinched, began tapping in the information. After she'd hit the send button, she slumped back into her chair, unable to look at anyone.

"We are all here for you, Victoria," Lizzie said gently, patting Victoria's shoulder.

Chapter Forty-Eight

Lizzie

Lizzie took one look at Cathy on her doorstep and knew the poor woman was overwrought. She hadn't combed her hair and was wearing baggy sweatpants that resembled brown potato sacks. The woman had never been much for appearance, but she was usually neat and clean.

After Lizzie'd settled Cathy into her most comfy chair, she went into the kitchen and put the kettle on and hurried back with a gentle smile on her face, worried Cathy's health had taken a turn for the worse, even though she'd seemed on the road to recovery after her operation.

Tom, Lizzie's sweet old cat seemed to sense Cathy was upset and jumped into her lap, settling himself across her knees.

"Is everything all right?" Lizzie patted Cathy's shoulder.

Cathy's face turned bright red. "Do you know if Victoria heard back from the sister?"

"Why don't you ask her yourself?" Lizzie had no intention of becoming their go-between.

"I can't," Cathy wailed. "I am so ashamed of having pushed her into seeking out the sister and her potential son. What if it isn't him? And what if it is? She shouldn't have to donate her kidney. I must have caused her to relive so many horrible memories." She grimaced. "I hate myself."

Lizzie remembered only too well when her ex, whose name she wished she could erase from her memory forever, made her hate herself as if she was as useless and unworthy as he'd once made her feel. In spite of how irritating Cathy had been as if she thought she was everyone's saviour, Lizzie wanted to make her feel better. "I know you meant well, Cathy. But you should not have interfered. Still, no doubt everything will work out for the best. And you did apologise. So, it's time to forgive yourself."

"I can't!" Cathy moaned. "Dear God! It was not my business to interfere in Victoria's life."

Lizzie, watching Cathy scratching the cat's knobby head, was reminded of how she'd revealed that she talked to her cat. Didn't everyone! "Maybe you can talk to Tom," she said with a smile hoping to lighten the mood, but one look at Cathy's unamused face, made her wish she'd kept her mouth shut.

"I'll fetch the tea," she said, eager to escape Cathy's obvious distress.

She soon returned with two mugs of hot tea and handed one to Cathy. The cat jumped down and wound around her legs. "Look, Cathy," she said, "it isn't as if you've done anything really terrible. In fact, you may have inadvertently set in motion something therapeutic for Victoria."

"Poor Victoria." Cathy stared at her teacup. "It must be awful to live such a lie for so many years. You didn't even know about her child, right?"

"No, she never told me. She was always private and never revealed much about her life."

"I've hidden a secret for years too. I am deeply ashamed of myself."

"You don't have to tell me!" Lizzie cried. "We've all done things we regret."

Cathy hesitated and took a sip of her tea to moisten her throat. "When I was twenty-five, my parents told me I was adopted. I was so angry with them. I had no desire to know who my birth mother was…"

"It must have hurt," Lizzie sympathised.

"It did hurt, so much so that I shut out my parents, who'd been nothing but good to me, all of my life. I felt betrayed. I was so stupid. And there's no way for me to make amends with them. They both died years ago." She sat her cup on the side table and put her hands over her face and began weeping.

Lizzie's eyes filled with tears too as she waited quietly for Cathy to stop crying and handed her a tissue. "Would you want to find your birth mother now?" she asked.

"God no!" Cathy said. "I don't want to open up that avenue of potential horrors."

"Perhaps," Lizzie said thoughtfully, "you should consider talking to a counsellor to help you let go of the past. My boss, the lady pastor at my church, is kind and also a trained therapist. You could talk things out with her."

"It was awful," Cathy said, staring into space. "I'd just begun nursing and was dating a doctor who I thought was the *One*. What a fool I was! What a fool! I'd expected him to be supportive when I told him about being adopted, but do you know what he said?"

Lizzie shook her head.

"He told me he could only be with someone he knew had good genetics and then he dumped me."

"What a creep!"

"Oh, there's more! He worked at the same hospital as me, and he was seeing the girl I thought was my best friend. I was devastated. I felt as if everyone at the hospital was laughing at me. I mean she was my best friend! I probably introduced them. I was always an outsider, even in primary school."

"You're not to blame for what happened with that guy. He didn't deserve you!" Lizzie didn't know what else to say.

"I know *now* that I didn't deserve what happened with him, but coupled with what I thought was my parents' betrayal, I quit my job and moved to the other side of London, here in Ickenham, where I ended up working as a receptionist for thirty years until the physician retired."

"Didn't you say you've been applying to hospitals for nursing jobs?"

"No one will hire me. The only nursing I did at the doctor's office was weigh people and ask them why they wanted to see him. I was a file clerk and scheduler. My nursing skills never got used." She groaned. "I'd loved being on the hospital wards actually taking care of patients, but I'm totally out of practice."

"You could probably take a refresher course. I certainly would if I had your education."

"Maybe, but I'm broke. And I haven't been in a classroom for years!"

"How about temping somewhere? Victoria got me a temporary job at St. Thomas while a woman was on maternity leave. It helped me financially, and it also helped my self-esteem. When the job ended I had the courage to seek a sexton job in the church where I now worship. I didn't know anything about building maintenance, but I figured I could learn. Now I do more than vacuum rugs. I take care of getting in all supplies and also hire contractors for repairs."

Cathy reached over and stroked Tom. "I so wanted to help other people, but I've been a dismal failure."

"Nonsense!" Lizzie vigorously shook her head. "We all deserve second chances! Just ask Lou!" She chuckled and Cathy half-smiled.

"Listen Cathy. Victoria hasn't worked in the hospital for a while ever since she inherited money from her aunt, but she might still have contacts. And she could point you in the right direction for refresher courses in nursing. And maybe if she hears from the sister she can get her DNA tested and find out if she is this sick man's mother. She will probably be grateful to you. It could be a win-win, right?"

Chapter Forty-Nine

Charlotte

Charlotte placed her coffee on the table beside her laptop and sighed. She was still reeling from the way Cathy had interfered in Victoria's business. What right did she have to contact the sister of that poor young man? But then, she thought pensively, it had given Victoria that push she needed to make contact. Maybe a gentle nudge in the right direction wasn't such a bad thing.

She wondered if Victoria had heard anything back from the sister, and if she were a match would she really donate a kidney? Charlotte knew, as a mother herself, she would give her right arm if it meant keeping her child alive, but this wasn't the same, was it? Victoria had no bond, no relationship with this man, her son. There was still a connection though, surely? An inherent link, bound by genetics and maternal instinct?

She made a mental note to cook a nice meal for her kids later. She wanted, no, *needed*, to catch up with them. So much had happened, what with their father being ill and then her running off to Scotland to find Colin. She felt like she hardly knew what was going on in their lives.

Gazing into nothingness, Charlotte sipped her drink, the rich caffeine warming her throat.

The brushing of little Mirabelle against her leg made her glance down, a smile of affection on her face. "Hello, my darling," she murmured, then chuckled as she was reminded of the conversation with the other ladies about talking to their cats. "Well, I think it's therapeutic talking to you, my sweet," she reached down to stroke the soft fur of her little friend. "Maybe you could help nudge me in the right direction, hey?"

She suddenly froze, her hand pausing mid stroke as clarity struck. It was time; she had to make a decision. For too long now she had dawdled and dithered, her life in limbo, waiting and searching for Colin. Colin, who she had now miraculously found, thanks to the help of the other ladies. Colin, who now wanted to try again, give themselves a second chance. But why? And if he genuinely still loved her, why did she have to find him? Why didn't he just come home?

Perhaps, she thought, depressingly, he'd never loved her at all. Maybe she was just a means to an end. After all, hadn't he told Ruthie he was waiting to sell his marital home? Correction: *her* home!

An unfamiliar rage suddenly erupted from the normally gentle Charlotte and with it a steely determination. *I am not a pushover, Colin! I believe in second chances, absolutely! But not our second chance, honey! Oh no, this is my second chance!*

Before she could change her mind, she tapped out a text to Lou.

Get me on that damn show of yours now!

She giggled softly and then opened her laptop to connect to the search engine, and with nimble and determined fingers she entered '*family divorce lawyers.*' Then she waited for the myriad of local solicitor firms to begin downloading.

Laughter burst from her, and she held her hand to her chest. "Free at last!" she muttered, and with her head stretched back so that her neck was strained, she howled, her mirth so liberating she emitted a snort that sent poor Mirabelle fleeing for cover.

Chapter Fifty

Lizzie

Lizzie couldn't wait for the cat ladies to arrive so she could tell them her new plans. With Bill!

She'd got them all settled in her sitting room with full glasses of wine before she began. "I have some exciting news to tell you gals. I'd like your opinion as to whether it's a good idea."

Victoria rolled her eyes as if she already knew but she didn't, and Lizzie chuckled, realising she was about to surprise them all. But Lou took centre stage. As per usual! She dipped her finger into her wine and ran it around the rim of her wine glass trying to make it ring. It didn't, but she'd managed to get everyone's attention.

Lizzie took a sip of wine and decided to wait for Lou to begin and end!

"I expect you've all seen my latest show with Charlotte and Colin. It was easy to bring Colin down from Scotland. He needed no convincing. But I should have realised Charlotte was suddenly a little too pleased to see the man, or so I thought. As you all no doubt know, Charlotte, on *live* TV, I repeat *live* TV, told Colin to fuck off and she handed him her solicitor's divorce application and told him she never wanted to see him again."

"Good for you, Charlotte," Victoria cried. "The man was a creep."

"He was," Cathy agreed. "You're doing the right thing. Who needs a lying bastard!"

Lou eyed Charlotte. "Yeah, I agree no one needs a lying...what did *you* call him, Charlotte? On *live* TV."

"A son of a bitch and I don't care if he was lying or not about working off the Great Barrier Reef trying to restore the corals. He could have told me! Three fucking years he was gone and to think I was fretting and worrying about him being hurt. For all I know, he has another wife out there, and kids. He only wants me back to get hold of half the money I'd get for the house. But it's mine, and he's not getting a penny. My lawyer is making sure of that!"

Lou made a face. "However, Charlotte, your unwelcome tirade on my show about second chances, as you know, caused the producers to cancel my program. So, thank you very much!"

Charlotte shrugged. "I'm sorry, Lou. That wasn't my intention. Is there any way I can make it up to you?"

"Probably not, but it has opened other doors for me, some of which I'll get to later. The thing is your words went viral, and the producers want me to emcee another show encouraging angry exes to have it out with one another."

"That sounds dreadful," Lizzie said. "Destructive."

"Probably," Lou agreed. "But enough about me. Who wants to go next? Cathy, you look as if you've swallowed an angry lizard. Anything you want to speak the truth about?"

"Lizzie," Cathy said, staring at Lizzie. "You promised not to tell!"

"I didn't tell," Lizzie responded.

"Aha!" Lou pounced. "I knew when you tried to get Victoria's son in touch with her, there was more to the story. Spill!" she demanded.

Lizzie interrupted before Cathy, who was staring sheepishly at her feet, could speak. "Let's have a bit of good news, for a change," she said and waited until they all nodded. "Raise your glasses. I want to celebrate!"

"For God's sake. We all know you and Bill are..."

"Are what, Victoria?"

"Getting married. I thought you'd have learned from your past horrible marriage to stay away from men."

"First off, Bill is not at all like my ex. But you're wrong. I have no intention of remarrying anyone. Bill is a practicing solicitor, and he's offered me a job a good paying one where I'll get to use my brains and not merely climb on ladders to change lightbulbs in the church where I work. Not that there is anything wrong with manual labour. As a matter of fact, I've learned a lot about fixing things. And I haven't needed a guy to take care of me. But with Bill, it's different..."

Victoria snorted and almost upset her wine.

Charlotte, ever the voice of reason, smiled at Lizzie. "If you are going to be Bill's secretary, that could be tricky."

Lizzie chuckled. "Of course not. I'm not going to end up lying across a desk. Bill makes me smile because he's funny, but I am not about to hop in bed with him. No," she took a big slug of her wine. "I'm going to be a paralegal as his assistant."

Charlotte looked puzzled. "Don't you have to have a degree and know the law?"

"As it turns out, I can work for Bill while I take online courses to qualify. It only takes about a year. And then I can get a job in other law offices too. And I'll have experience."

Cathy piped up, "That's wonderful, Lizzie." She raised her glass. "To second chances!"

They chinked their wine glasses and said cheers!

Charlotte was happy for her friend, and then she glanced at Lou who was a little too bright-eyed. Even for her. "You said, Lou, there was something else you had to tell?"

Lou, ever the actress, took a drawn-out moment for effect. She grinned. "As you know, Ruthie is selling her B & B. Mac and I are going to buy it!"

Victoria snorted, yet again, except louder than before and she started to laugh. "You!" she said, pointing at Lou's high heels. "You, cleaning toilets is too funny to imagine!"

The others tried not to snicker but were clearly repressing their surprise along with their mirth.

"That doesn't sound practical," Charlotte said.

"I'm not going to live there!" Lou smiled knowingly. "It's going to be an investment. Mac will take over for a while, and if my *Mean Men* show doesn't work out for any length of time, I'll eventually move up there with him! To bonnie Scotland! I might start wearing kilts," she joked.

"You hardly know him!" Cathy cried, wiping her eyes, as she proceeded to tell them about the doctor who'd left her and ruined her chances of practicing nursing in a hospital. "Don't do something you'll regret!"

Victoria nodded thoughtfully. "We've all got some serious decisions to make. You seem to be the only one who has made up her mind, Charlotte.

Lizzie has to decide if it would be wise to go work for a guy who fancies her. Cathy, you could get into hospital nursing if you chose to take some catch up courses. I'm fairly sure there's grant money available, so that's something for you to consider. Lou, are you sure you want to run a show that pits people against one another? And how do you know Mac is sincere? He might be after more than your body. Money, for instance."

Everyone looked expectantly at Victoria, who was now staring at the wall, her piece said. Lizzie piped up, "What about you, Victoria? Are you any closer to your important decision?"

She shook her head. "I don't know what to do! How am I to get a DNA test from him without revealing I am his mother and how he was conceived? It might destroy him!"

Chapter Fifty-One

Victoria

Victoria sat down anxiously at the table in the coffee shop, having just ended her frantic phone call with Cathy, a conversation she had already forgotten. When the young waitress arrived to take her order, she felt momentarily confused and was startled. "Just a latte for now, please." She looked nervously around, but the café was empty aside from two teenage girls occupying a table at the back, giggling over their phones and paying no attention to the older woman, Victoria, sitting stiffly, her eyes wide, her heart hammering.

Her stomach churned, though not with hunger; Lord knows she had no appetite these days, especially today.

For today was the day she'd find out if the young man in need of a kidney was indeed her son. At any moment, a young woman, his sister, Natalie, would walk through the door and with her the results of the DNA test that would determine her future.

Victoria, emboldened by Charlotte's firm decision to divorce Colin, and Lou's ambition, albeit fanciful, to buy Ruth's B&B, as well as Lizzie and Cathy focusing on their careers, had bitten the bullet and sent a heartfelt and honest message to Natalie:

I hope you believe this message is genuine and I'm sorry I've squandered some precious time in coming to this decision, but I truly needed to explore my feelings, as well as consider those of you and your brother.

I had a son years ago, the same age as your brother, that I gave up for adoption for reasons that I am not ready to discuss. I was only a child myself and the decision to give him up was, sadly, not mine to make. However, I have thought about that boy every day of my life. If there is a chance, any chance, that I am his mother and could, therefore, donate a kidney, then I am willing to do whatever it takes to make it happen.

I hope to hear back from you soon…

From the moment Victoria had sent the message, there had been a flurry of exchanges between herself and Natalie, and they had concluded that until they were sure Victoria was a DNA match with Ben, they would keep it between them.

Victoria had bought a DNA testing kit, taken her swabs, sealed them and sent them to Natalie, who then added a sample of her brother, Ben's hair and sent them off.

Now, Victoria waited for Natalie to arrive and confirm if Ben was indeed her son.

Ben, Victoria thought with a smile. She liked that name; it sounded gentle but strong. She wondered if he'd like her, then silently admonished herself. She was getting carried away, imagining saving her son and them forging a wonderful relationship! She didn't even know him! Didn't even know if he was her son yet!

The café door swung open, and an attractive young blonde lady entered, glancing at the giggly teens, then focusing on Victoria, a tentative smile on her face.

"Natalie?" Victoria stood to greet her, her legs almost giving way.

"Victoria, are you okay?" Natalie dashed to her side and gently pushed her back into her seat.

"Sorry, sorry…" Victoria began.

"It's fine," Natalie soothed, "I'm nervous too, and I'm not the one about to find my long-lost son…"

"So, it's a match!" Victoria almost screeched the words, but Natalie was shaking her head. "Wait, no, no, sorry I should have worded that better. I haven't looked yet since we agreed we'd open the results together. I just meant you might be about to find your long-lost son."

Victoria blew out her cheeks, not sure if she was disappointed it wasn't confirmed yet, or because they still had to do the terrifying task of opening the results.

"Would you like a tea or coffee before we find out?" Victoria asked as her latte was placed in front of her.

Natalie shook her head. "Let's just get this over with, shall we?"

Victoria gulped and slowly nodded her agreement.

Chapter Fifty-Two

Cathy

After Cathy answered Victoria's garbled phone call about her DNA, she took a cab to the coffee shop in Wembley where her friend was with the potential son's sister. She wished the driver would race around the stalled traffic and go faster, but there was no way to speed up things.

While they were inching along, she called Lizzie and told her about Victoria, adding, "I can't imagine why she called me and not you."

Lizzie groaned. "She called you probably because you are a nurse. What's the name of that coffee shop? I'll come immediately."

"You'd better take the Tube. Traffic is backed up."

After thirty minutes, the traffic began to move faster, and the cab soon dropped her off in front of the café. She quickly paid the driver, telling him to keep the change, not caring she'd given him far too much for the tip. She didn't care if it was her last twenty pounds, and she had no way to even pay for a Tube home. Over the years, she'd done her best to stop acting rashly but she'd jumped at the opportunity to be a help, especially to Victoria.

She hesitated, hoping Lizzie might have gotten here before her, but when she looked inside the darkened shop, at the back were a couple of girls scrolling on their phones and off to her right at a nearby table she spotted Victoria, with her back to her, facing a blonde woman. No Lizzie. For a few moments she stood in the doorway, light from outside casting her shadow onto the floor.

"Have a seat," a girl called from behind the bar. "I'll be with you in a sec."

Victoria spun around. "Cathy," she cried. "You came!"

"Of course," she answered and approached the table. "Lizzie's coming too."

The blonde woman pulled over a chair for her. "I'm Natalie, Ben's sister," she said. "I'm so glad you're here for Victoria. This has been quite a shock."

Cathy, observing Victoria's pale face, was at a loss for words. Should she come right out and ask if the DNA was a match?

Natalie smiled gently and took matters into her own hands. "The DNA has confirmed that Victoria is my brother Ben's mother. Isn't that wonderful?"

Cathy wasn't sure if it was so wonderful, but she was here to support Victoria no matter what. Since it might help Victoria to have more medical information, she'd spent some time refreshing herself about kidney transplants. Before she said a word, Victoria reached across the table and took her hand, managing to knock her cup of cold latte over, spilling it everywhere.

Cathy grabbed some napkins and threw them over the liquid. The barista hurried over with a roll of paper towels and mopped up the coffee and dried the table. She patted Victoria's back. "No worries," she said. "I'll get you all fresh cups. On the house."

Obviously, the woman must have heard their conversation. "How very kind. That would be great."

At last Victoria managed to croak, "I am not sure how I feel. I've longed for my son to be in my life, but how will he feel if he finds out what happened?"

The sister looked puzzled. "You were only thirteen. It doesn't matter. All that matters now is if you are willing to donate a kidney."

"I am! I will!" Victoria cried. "But it's probably best if Ben never finds out about me!"

Cathy knew from the stricken look on Victoria's face that she was heartbroken to have found her son and yet be unable to actually get to meet him. "I'm a nurse," she told Natalie to give credence to what she was about to say. "There is no guarantee Victoria will be an acceptable donor even though she and Ben are related. It's possible they will have different blood types. Not only that, Victoria, you will have to go through many tests including psychological evaluation."

Victoria and Natalie both looked so crestfallen that she felt as if she'd thrown cold water in their faces.

Before she continued to give possibly unwanted medical advice, their drinks were put on the table, along with three chocolate biscotti. "You ladies, take your time," the barista said. "Chocolate might help!"

Victoria erupted into uneasy laughter. "Oh my God, it'll take more than chocolate to solve this dilemma and make things right!"

"But," Natalie said, "we're on the right track."

"Yes," Cathy added. "And even if you're not able to be Ben's donor directly, it is possible to donate anonymously and you can be what's called a paired donor so someone else who is compatible can give his or her kidney to Ben, and yours goes to someone else who needs one."

The door swung open and Lizzie, flushed from running, hurried over and wrapped her arms around Victoria.

"I'll be all right," Victoria whispered, and Lizzie let her go and pulled a chair over to their little round table.

"I'm Natalie," Ben's sister said. "My brother is in Guy's Hospital. They have an excellent kidney donor program with almost a hundred percent success rate. Ben has already signed up for a kidney. So, Victoria, that's the place to go. Ben is on the Richard Bright ward. I'm going there now if you want to come with me and get signed up with the specialist. I've already apprised her that I might have found you, Ben's mother, I'm sure she'll race you through the process." With raised eyebrows, she scanned Victoria's face questioningly. "He looks like you," she added. "Same nose and same eyes."

Lizzie shrugged. "Victoria, you need to take time to make your decision."

"I have and I am going ahead to help my..." she hesitated before saying, "my son." Turning to Natalie, she said. "I'll come with you now."

"I'll fetch my car and pick you up outside." Natalie stood up, opened her purse and threw a fiver on the table. "Be back in a minute."

"I'll be happy to come with you," Cathy offered Victoria.

"No," Victoria said. "You've already helped enough. I'll give you my keys so you can feed my cat if they put me in the hospital right away."

A white Mercedes soon pulled up outside. Victoria grabbed her purse, tossed a ring of keys on the table, went outside and climbed into the passenger side.

"Dear God," Lizzie said, watching the car pull away from the curb. "I certainly hope it works out for everyone."

"Me too," Cathy answered. "I wish I could have gone along but I know Guys Hospital has the best specialists." She took a sip of her coffee, wondering how to broach borrowing money from Lizzie to pay for her fare home. It was so embarrassing. As she gathered Victoria's keys to put in her purse, she was tempted to grab the fiver. If Lizzie questioned her, she could pretend she didn't realise what she'd done.

She took the fiver and examined it. "Gosh, this is almost brand new," she remarked. It was sorely tempting, but she knew she ought to ask for help, something she hated to do. But Lizzie would no doubt despise her for stealing the barista's tip far more than the fact she needed to borrow a couple of quid. Gosh, if all those years ago she hadn't worried so much about what people thought of her, she might still be nursing. She put the fiver back, wishing she could add another couple of quid.

Chapter Fifty-Three

Cathy

As Cathy made her way down the long hallway in Guys Hospital, she found herself remembering when she'd been a nurse so many years ago, or at least a proper nurse and not a receptionist. It seemed odd that *now* she was thinking back. When she'd recently been in the hospital for her operation, she hadn't thought along these lines. Instead, she'd appreciated the kindness of her nurses and the skill of her doctor. Maybe her current anxiety about the past was her having recently told Lizzie what happened with that deceptive doctor she thought was going to marry her, and his nasty rejection. Oh, dear God, what if he worked in *this* hospital now and she ran into him?

She stopped, momentarily startled by her racing heart and panic, but there was no way that man would recognise her! She'd once been slim and pretty, but was old now, much fatter, and didn't feel a bit feminine. For some reason, she didn't care if she did meet that old nurse friend who'd been his apparent great love with great genetics. She was probably fat and had bad teeth now! Cathy almost laughed out loud at such mean thoughts. She shifted the small bunch of flowers she'd brought for Victoria and nodded to a nurse going into a patient's room, reminded of how much she would love to be in her shoes. She certainly needed a job.

She stood in the entrance to Victoria's private room and was deeply aware that she was not the one in need of care but had come to offer comfort to Victoria just as she'd hoped to do on the ward where she'd once worked when she'd started her nursing career. She'd worked in the ICU, as well as on open wards where patients did not need specialised care. She'd helped all of her patients and their families by supporting them as well as administering their meds. Some of them had temporary urinary catheters such as the one snaking from under the sheets on the bed where Victoria reclined against some pillows with her eyes closed.

Cathy hated to disturb her, but as she placed the flowers on the cross-bed table, Victoria opened her eyes. "Hello, Cathy," she said, sounding quite strong.

Cathy turned, smiling. "How are you feeling?"

"Relieved to have this over with, that's for sure."

Cathy nodded. "Of course. Who wouldn't be? You look well, though, and once you've rested, you'll be back to normal in no time."

"The doctor said she wants me to stay in hospital for a few more days to make sure I don't get pneumonia or develop high blood pressure." She half-smiled and pressed the call button for assistance.

"Are you all right?" Cathy asked. "Let me help you."

"I feel fine but thought you might like a vase and water for the lovely flowers."

Cathy wished she'd been able to afford something better than this small bunch of daisies, especially upon noticing a large bouquet of red roses dotted with delicate white baby's breath on the windowsill.

"They're from my son, Ben. And *no,* he doesn't know the donor was his mother. And I want to keep it that way. His sister, Natalie, has promised to say nothing."

Cathy hesitated but this was no time for a real friend to keep silent. "Years ago," she said, "I let what other people thought of me cause me to make my decision to leave nursing and I've regretted it for years. Don't make that mistake and lose the opportunity to get to know your son."

"I want to know my son!" Victoria cried. "But I can't! What will he think to discover his parentage? It might destroy him! I haven't told his sister Natalie the circumstances of his conception other than I was very young and would have kept him if I'd been older!"

"You are so brave, Victoria! You could tell him you don't know who the father was. After all you are giving him his life a second time."

"I hope so! I'd as soon pretend he was the result of a loving relationship with an older boy. But the problem is I've filed a report about having been raped and given the names of my cousins."

"How awful for you but you were right to turn them in. Who knows who else they might have abused."

"I know. I should have filed a report years ago. Oh well. Better late than never." She looked thoughtful. "If you don't mind my asking, have you decided what to do about nursing?"

Cathy filled her in, adding sadly, "I'd love to be a nurse again, but doubt if I have the stamina or ability to learn new techniques, let alone operate all these specialised medical instruments." She stared at the monitor with its flashing measurements on display.

"Nonsense," Victoria said. "You're not too old. And you're smart! You need a refresher course or two. Hand me that pen and notepad, please. I'll give you the phone number of a guy I used to work with. He's an administrator at Lewisham Hospital. I bet he can set you on the right path and probably get you some grant money if that would help. Or I'd be glad to loan you the money. I inherited quite a sum from the aunt who protected her nasty sons rather than me. She took them to Australia. I was glad to hear she'd died and the money she left me was obviously guilt money. I'd like nothing better to use it to help my friends."

While she was looking up the number on her mobile phone and scribbling it down, the door was pushed open.

Cathy expected to see a nurse answering the call button, but instead her eyes grew wide, and her mouth fell open to see a man sitting in the wheelchair that Natalie was pushing.

Chapter Fifty-Four

Lou

If ever there was a second chance miracle, this was it, Lou thought, hurriedly tapping her phone screen with a message to her producer: *I have the perfect second chance story for you! Please, just reinstate my show! It doesn't even have to be about romantic relationships. The scoop I have for you is mind-blowing!*

She waited for the little dots to appear, heralding a response, but nothing came.

Damn! They really were freezing her out. Now that the *Mean Men* show idea had been cancelled, all because of some woke TV exec who thought it sexist and sensationalist to expose love cheats live on tv – *huh, what the hell?* Lou was now desperate to get some or any kind of airtime!

The phone in her hand rang out and startled her, but she quickly accepted the call. "Mac, darling," she purred.

Mac wasted no time in getting down to business. "Lou, the sale has fallen through on the B&B."

Lou's heart turned to sand. "What? Why? The money is there; the bank was instructed to release it just this morning. I don't understand." As she spoke, Lou's pulse raced, her throat became dry, and previous cautions from the other cat ladies rose in her memory: *He could just be with you for your money...*

"Lou, did *you* hear me?"

Casting her mind back to the present moment, Lou muttered a "hmm?"

"It's nothing to do with the money, your money is still with the bank."

"So, what...?"

"Ruth has decided she doesn't want to sell. She's keeping the B&B, and, get this, she's taking on a partner to help her run it! You'll never guess who!"

Lou's mouth gaped open. "Who?"

Mac chuckled at the end of the line, irritating Lou beyond belief.

"Who, Mac?" she asked sternly.

"Bloody Charlotte, hahaha!"

Lou stared at her phone. What the hell? Was Mac drunk? "Mac, sorry, what did you say? Because I'm not really understanding this."

Mac, clearly struggling to get over his mirth at the turn of events, finally calmed down enough to respond. "Yes, sweet Lou. Oh, so perfect, whimsical, Charlotte has decided she and Ruthie are going to run the B&B together."

As Mac broke into further maniacal laughter, Lou slapped her hand to her mouth. *What on Earth?* "Mac," she finally replied, "I'm completely blindsided, I'll call you back."

"Don't bother," was Mac's reply as he hung up on her.

Lou looked at her phone. *What just happened?* She quickly clicked on Charlotte's number, waiting as the call rang out. Next, she chose Victoria's number. "Lou," was the cold greeting. "Victoria, how are you Doll?" Lou regained her usual composure.

"How am I?" Lou winced at the tone in Victoria's voice.

"How am I? Seeing as I just heard your plan to put my whole personal life on your second chance show, you mean?"

Lou froze, "What? But how?"

"How did I know?" Victoria interrupted her. "Your producer, Derek, had the good grace to let me know that's how!"

"Wait," Lou was confused. "How do you know my Derek, you never even…"

"Met him?" Victoria finished for her. "Oh, but I have, Lou, other than that one brief and disastrous time on your silly show. You see, Lizzie's Bill got on quite well with him, they kept in touch, and he just told me your diabolical plan. Thanks again for your concern, by the way."

Lou sighed, and her face flushed. "I'm sorry I didn't get the chance to visit you, I was tied up with the B&B, speaking of which, did you hear that Charlotte…"

Before Lou could continue, Victoria spoke, her tone sharp. "I don't care for your gossip about Charlotte, all I know, from Derek, is that you were happy to expose my life to millions. I know Lizzie is happy with Bill, as I might one day be with someone. I know Cathy is finally back into her nurse training, and ready to re-establish her career, and finally I know that you, Lou…"

Lou heard Victoria's voice quiver as she took a long deep breath before continuing.

"You, Lou, are the most self-centered, narcissistic person, I know. Please do not contact me again."

After the second call of the day was cancelled on her, Lou sunk into the armchair, her body trembling with the shock of Victoria's angry words. The furless skinny body of Peregrine rubbed against her ankles, and she looked down at her little guy. "Oh Peregrine," she moaned, placing her head in her hands, as the tears streamed down her face. "What have I done?"

Chapter Fifty-Five

Charlotte

Charlotte glanced at the wall clock and grabbed her keys just as her doorbell began chiming repeatedly and someone began rapping on the door. *Who on earth?* she thought and hurried to answer. To her surprise and annoyance there stood Lou, looking bedraggled in sweatpants and a matching top that looked as if it needed a wash.

"What do you want?" she barked, not wanting anything to do with Lou.

"Can I come in?" Lou pleaded.

"No. I'm on my way to the airport to pick up Ruth and I'm already late!"

"I'll come with you!" Lou's eyes begged and Charlotte, kind as always, nodded okay, stepped outside past Lou, slammed and locked her front door and hurried, with Lou trailing behind, to her car parked one street over.

Once they were on the road, Lou cleared her throat, "Ahem. I'm glad about you and Ruthie. She's a lovely lady."

"What are you talking about Lou?" Charlotte replied, sounding as cross as she felt at having been waylaid by Lou.

"Mac told me about you and Ruthie becoming partners."

Charlotte shot her a sideways glance before bursting into laughter. "You are out of your mind. Partners? Ruthie is coming to stay with me for a few days while she looks for a flat here in London. She wants to be closer to her kids and grandkids. As for me, Scotland is not in the offing for me. For one thing, I'd hate to run into Colin or give him any ideas. For another, I love teaching and am getting my curriculum ready for the next semester. So, I don't know what you're going on about with Ruthie and I!"

Charlotte slowed down for a red light and stopped the car. "Ruth sold her B & B to Mac. I thought that was the plan."

Lou absorbed these words for a while feeling confused, wondering if Mac had intentionally been having her on. *Jerk*, she thought, wondering if she ought to check her bank account and put a hold on any transactions.

Neither said a word until they drove into the short-term car park at London Heathrow and Charlotte spoke into her phone. "Is your plane here yet, Ruth?"

"Just landed and taxiing to the exit," came the reply over the Bluetooth car connection.

"Great! We'll meet you in baggage claim and help you with your bags."

"Thanks, Charlotte. Are the other cat ladies with you?" There was a smile in her voice.

"Only Lou." Charlotte expertly pulled in between two cars and undid her seatbelt.

"Put Lou on!" Ruth's voice was no longer friendly but serious.

"We're on speaker phone," Charlotte alerted her.

"Good, because I want a word with you Lou!"

Lou slumped in her seat and muttered okay.

"First of all, your treatment of Mac was outrageous, leading him on the way you did. And secondly, how could you possibly think Victoria would be okay with you exposing her newly found son to the whole world for your personal gain? You ought to be ashamed of yourself!"

"I am," Lou said quietly.

"Then you need to publicly apologise to Mac, to Victoria, and to everyone else you've hurt through your lack of concern for others. There is no excuse."

"I know," Lou whispered.

"Well, I've got to turn off my phone. I'll be glad to see you, Charlotte!"

"I'll wait here," Lou told Charlotte. "I've got a call to make."

Charlotte didn't care who Lou was calling and was glad she didn't come to baggage claim. It took about thirty minutes before she and Ruth arrived back at the car and stowed Ruth's two wheelies into the trunk.

Lou had climbed into the back seat. "I want to make amends," Lou said, her voice shaking.

"I should hope so," Ruth retorted, quickly buckling her seat belt.

"I went on Tik Tok and have posted a public apology," Lou muttered.

"You did what?" Charlotte cried, feeling as if she'd been kicked in the stomach, and fearing the worst.

"Listen," Lou said, and tapped the Tik Tok app into her phone to display her with tears running down her face.

Charlotte suspected these crocodile tears were all part of an act, but she listened carefully to Lou's somber voice.

"Everyone," Lou spoke. *"I have made a big mistake and alienated everyone I love. My book club friends are probably going to disown me, including Victoria who I wanted to bring on my show as a help to her and the son she has just connected with after forty odd years. I only meant to help with Second Chance Saloon, but all of my TV shows have been cancelled. Now I am the one who needs a second chance."* She wiped her nose with a tissue. *"But maybe it's not all my fault. I mean it's obvious a thirteen-year-old girl wouldn't get herself pregnant with her cousins on purpose, right? Still, these days with all the sex on TV, who knows what kids are up to? I mean nowadays there's way too much graphic sex, leaving nothing to the imagination. Except for the guys. Men are so full of themselves and their precious dicks! You've only got to see that ad about their bent carrots causing them so much concern."* She chuckled.

Charlotte and Ruth both gasped. "Delete that immediately," Charlotte ordered. "Dear God, you had no right to reveal to the world anything so personal. Besides Victoria's son doesn't know anything about his birth."

"How was I to know? And I can't take it down now. It's already gone viral. Please hear the rest of the video." Her voice droned on: *"I am so sorry for how I've hurt people. I only hope everyone will forgive me. I pledge to donate all the money I earned from my recent shows to Save the Children, and I hope many of you will be able to match my contribution. It's over a hundred thousand pounds. By all means choose another charity to help. Maybe Oxfam. Something like that. Thank you for hearing me out!"*

Charlotte threw Ruth a glance and rolled her eyes.

"For God's sake," Ruth muttered. "Lou, you are such a drama queen! How do you suppose anyone can match that huge amount of money? Maybe instead of such a ridiculous gesture, you should donate a hundred quid and set up a GoFundMe account on Facebook. If you actually give away all of your money, I doubt you'd survive being homeless for long. And let's face it, at your age, you probably can't offer call girl services to anyone either."

Lou groaned. "I want to make things right!"

"Then," Charlotte responded. "Why don't you start by going up to Inverness and talk directly to Mac."

Ruth intervened, "he told me he didn't trust Lou to be his partner, after the way she treated her friends. He said he felt she was leading him on, using him as a means to better herself, hence he bought the B&B with his own money without needing any of hers. Besides, it's hard work running a B & B what with changing bed linens, cleaning bathrooms, hoovering, dusting, preparing breakfasts, and generally being pleasant to people who might be rude and demanding."

"Look, what you did was wrong, Lou," Charlotte added. "Perhaps you need to take time to think about what *you* really want. Are you willing to give up your acting career to become an Innkeeper or did you simply want a way out after the failure of your show? I'm sorry, I don't mean to be brutal, but you need to be realistic."

"I thought Mac was *The One* for me! I expected us to be great together. He seemed supportive and kind…"

"Then why did you ignore his calls and messages?" Ruth interrupted.

"I'd had enough of guys using me!" Lou cried and filled them in about her married lover who'd finally left his wife for another woman, someone much younger than her, someone he'd taken to Hollywood.

"I know for a fact Mac is divorced," Ruth said, "so at least that wouldn't be a problem unless he went back to his wife."

Charlotte groaned and started the car. "Just go up and talk to the man and decide if you can make a serious commitment. You can lay some ground rules and maybe even get some therapy."

Lou threw open the car door and began clambering out.

Charlotte thought Lou must have lost her mind. "What are you doing?"

"I'm going to try to catch the plane that brought Ruth down from Inverness. It's probably going right back."

Charlotte sighed. "For God's sake, get back in the car and go home and pack some clothes."

"No need for clothes!" Lou cracked. "Men find me irresistible!" And with her handbag slung over her shoulder, looking like a bag-lady in her dirty sweat-clothes, she tore across the parking lot toward the terminal.

Chapter Fifty-Six

Victoria

Victoria winced as she gingerly swung her legs off the hospital bed, her newly scarred skin pulling against the stitches.

"You okay?" Natalie asked, concerned.

Victoria nodded resolutely, "abso-bloody-lutely! Ready to get home."

Natalie smiled sadly and looked downwards.

Victoria noticed, "but not before I see Ben. How is he?"

Natalie's face lit up. "He's so good! Obviously, it was a shock to hear about his conception, thanks to your friend…" Her face fell and Victoria interrupted.

"Trust me, she's no friend of mine now!" Victoria grimaced again, as she tried to put her arms through her cardigan.

"Here, let me help you," Natalie intervened, gently guiding Victoria into her clothes.

Victoria murmured her thanks and looked at Natalie, at a loss of what to say.

"You know…" Natalie began, and Victoria did too, "Look, I…"

They both chuckled and Victoria gestured to Natalie. "You go first."

Natalie smiled. "I think, if you're able to, Ben would really like to know what happened."

Victoria nodded her head thoughtfully. "It's something I've tried to bury for years, well, most of my life; except him, the baby, Ben…" She looked sheepishly to Natalie. "The abuse though, I mean, that's what I tried to bury."

Natalie swiped a tear from her face and grabbed Victoria's hand. "Tell my brother," She smiled sadly, "tell your son."

Victoria smiled and squeezed Natalie's hand back. "Well, you'd better wheel me up to the Reno ward then!" And with trepidation, yet quickly before she could change her mind, she left her hospital room to have a serious heart-to-heart with Ben. No, not Ben, her son.

Relief at finally getting to tell the truth filled her as Natalie pressed the button for the elevator up to the Reno ward.

"That's her!!!" Victoria's head spun at the roars coming from paparazzi down the corridor.

"Dear God," Natalie murmured.

"You're the abused child that gave birth to a child you just donated your kidney to!" someone yelled.

"Quick, quick!" Natalie cried at the lift to come sooner.

"Fucking Lou!" Victoria cursed as the elevator arrived in the nick of time as the reporters swarmed towards her. Natalie quickly rushed her and herself into it. "I'm gonna bloody kill her!"

"Not if I do first," Natalie seethed from clenched teeth.

As the doors slid shut, and the elevator rose, taking Victoria up to see her son, she still couldn't help but smile. Although they'd met after the kidney donation, because of the risk of infection, it had been a short visit. His gratitude had torn at her heart; Dear Lord, it was the least she could do!

But now, at last, she would speak to him about the reality of the situation. She only hoped he would understand. He'd been given the all-clear, although he would remain in hospital a while longer whilst they monitored his kidney function. And she was so ready to live again. After they'd talked.

And as soon as she could, she intended to let that bloody cow, Lou, have it! How dare she expose her and her son in such a manner to the whole damn world! How dare she! What a bloody self-centered bitch she was.

Lizzie'd told her to forgive the harm and wrongdoing done to her so she could let go of her bitterness. Could Lizzie be right? Maybe, just maybe, Lou, with all her highfalutin drama had actually done her a favour. Maybe Cathy, poking her unassuming nose into her business, had done the same.

Victoria smiled and breathed deeply.

"Are you sure you're okay?" Natalie asked, her voice full of concern, as the lift doors opened.

Victoria nodded.

"For the first time, in a very long time," she sighed, a serene smile on her face, "I actually am."

And as she was wheeled into her son's room, she knew it was true.

Chapter Fifty-Seven

Lizzie

Lizzie hit the off button on her phone and put it in her backpack that was slung over her office chair. She was surprised, to say the least, that Lou asked her—practically begged her—to come over to her flat after work. But since she wouldn't say what for, Lizzie could guess. Lou obviously needed a friend since her rushed trip to Scotland must have been a waste of time and she'd alienated everyone by betraying Victoria's confidence publicly on Tik Tok. No doubt, Lou stupidly didn't realise how easy it would be for people to figure out Victoria was the woman whose son had received her kidney.

After finishing her paperwork for Bill's latest lawsuit, she closed her laptop and stowed it in her backpack, quickly threaded her arms through the straps. "Goodnight, Bill. See you tomorrow!" she called into his office where he sat opposite a client. He waved and smiled.

With an umbrella raised she braved the steady rain and was tempted to call an Uber but decided a bus was much cheaper. She had just made it to the bus stop when a double-decker pulled up and she climbed aboard. This one went around the houses but within twenty minutes she was disembarking near Lou's place. She'd much rather have headed home. She had assignments to do for her online paralegal course, but Lou's desperation could not be ignored. Not that she deserved much empathy. Still, she was a person in need and Lizzie hoped she'd always be the sort of person to be a help.

Once she made it to Lou's place and rang the doorbell, it wasn't long before Lou appeared and took her dripping umbrella to sit it in a container near the door, then ushered Lizzie into the lounge and offered her a cup of tea. "Yes please," Lizzie answered, taking off her backpack before plopping down in a chair while Lou went to make the tea. The Manx cat jumped onto Lizzie's lap and curled up in a ball, purring loudly. "You're very pretty, Peridot," she murmured.

Lou came back with a pot of tea, milk and sugar, and two mugs on a tray. "His name's Peregrine," she said. "But he is a precious jewel to me, probably the only one who loves me!" She poured the tea. "I need your help, Lizzie," she remarked dolefully.

"What can I do?" Lizzie asked, hoping it wasn't another harebrained scheme.

"Would you give me a reference?"

"What!" Lizzie cried. "What for?"

Lou stared at her flat shoes which Lizzie noticed were brand new, so unlike her usual high heels. "I need a job. And Mac will have nothing to do with me, so I thought maybe if I proved to him that I am reliable and capable of domestic tasks, he'd reconsider letting me partner with him at the B & B."

"What exactly did he say?" Lizzie added milk and sugar to her tea and managed to stir it in without dislodging the cat.

"I haven't talked to him. I was going to show up on his doorstep in Inverness, but there were no connecting flights which was just as well, or he'd likely think of me as even more rash and thoughtless. I regret having ignored his earlier phone calls and I stood him up once. We were supposed to meet by the lions in Trafalgar Square, but I didn't go. I know I shouldn't have played hard to get, but I chased after that married guy for so many years, believing he loved me. I thought I loved him, but I didn't. After reflection, I realised I merely hoped he'd help my acting career. But clearly even when he did get me that hostess job and my own show, I blew it." She slumped in her chair. "I'm sorry. I'm rambling."

"It's okay," Lizzie responded. "I'm listening."

"The thing is my career is in shambles. I wanted to give my show earnings to Save the Children, but Ruth told me not to be stupid and end up homeless. I wanted to make amends to Victoria, but money won't undo the harm I caused for Victoria and all of the cats by exposing them to public scrutiny no one wanted."

Lizzie smiled ruefully. "You did introduce me to Bill and that's led me to new opportunities, and I don't only mean romantic ones. Bill is a good friend, too."

"I want more than friendship with Mac. He's a thoroughly decent guy. He wants to run a sanctuary for seals, ducks, whatever, when they are caught in nets or hurt in some way and need to be vetted."

"So, he's a vet?"

"No, but he can't stand innocent children or animals being abused. He no doubt thinks I abused Victoria. I didn't mean to!" Lou wailed.

"Of course you didn't," Lizzie said kindly. "You *were* thoughtless though and impulsive."

"That is why I am trying to be more measured. I'm tired of chasing men and acting jobs that hardly ever come through. I want something steady. Something normal."

"What sort of job? Cashier? Teacher's aide?"

"I wouldn't mind working in that church where you used to work. I am capable of vacuuming rugs, and I am good at fixing things. I'd be happy to wash and iron the vestments and robes or whatever is needed. And," she added with a smile. "I can play the piano. I'd need some practice to get me up to speed but maybe I could help out with hymn accompaniment."

"I'm not sure how normal working in a church is. In any case, my job didn't involve playing the piano. They have a music director for that, but you never know when they might need a sub. And you'd get to ring the bell. It doesn't pay much, but it helped me when I was desperate because it gave me a sense of purpose as well as a few quid to see me through the week."

Lou's face crumpled as if she might start crying. "I have enough money to keep me going for a while, but I am feeling depressed and useless. I want to be helpful! Somewhere!"

"Okay, I'll call the vicar and ask her if she needs a new Sexton and recommend you."

"Sexton," Lou muttered through giggles. "How appropriate!"

Lizzie giggled too. "A sexton is the name for a person who takes care of the church and its grounds. They used to be gravediggers too!"

Lou's eyes got big. "I couldn't do that!"

"These days they have backhoes for the job, so no worries there." She sat Peregrine on the floor and retrieved her phone from her backpack and entered a code for the church, "No answer," she said. "I'll try again later and let you know."

Chapter Fifty-Eight

Charlotte

"Cheers to the craziest few months of my life!" Charlotte clinked her wine glass to Ruthie's and sipped the golden nectar.

Ruthie chuckled and shook her head, "you couldn't make it up!" She raised her eyebrows and took a sip of her wine.

Charlotte smiled. "I'm afraid wherever Lou is involved, there'll always be a story."

Ruthie leaned forward and took Charlotte's hand. "She has redeemed herself though, you have to admit."

Charlotte was already nodding her agreement. "She really has. Who'd have thought, our vivacious buxom heroine would be getting her bachelor's degree in theology, so she might become an ordained minister?"

"I know!" Ruth was wide-eyed. "Fair play to her though, for turning her life around."

Charlotte sipped from her glass again. "It's wonderful, and that Victoria has found it in her heart to forgive her."

"Well forgiveness is the path to redemption, as they say."

Charlotte snorted the giggle that rose from her chest. "I'm not sure that's an actual saying, but hey, I'm sure it's true."

"You forgave Colin," Ruth gently reminded her.

Charlotte shrugged her shoulders. "I didn't take him back, but yes, I guess I did forgive. But I did that for myself, not him. The negativity was exhausting me."

"Speaking of which, do you think Mac will forgive Lou, give her another chance?"

"Oh, you didn't know? I thought I mentioned it. Mac and Lou are dating again."

"What the..." Ruth sat forward, "How did I not know this?"

Charlotte nodded animatedly. "Yep, taking it slow; he's obviously still cautious after her treatment of him, but it's a tentative start in the right direction."

"Well, cheers to that!" Ruth drained the rest of her wine. "Another?" she asked Charlotte, who shook her head.

"No, I have to get going, I'm meeting the kids for dinner."

"How lovely," Ruth murmured. "How long are they over for?"

"Just a few weeks, they're going home to spend Christmas in the States with their dad, but it's great to spend some time catching up without drama."

"I'll bet," Ruth agreed. "Where are you spending Christmas?"

"At home, and I was hoping you'd come to mine, if you don't have any plans?"

"Well, I'm not seeing my kids and grandkids till the new year, and until the purchase of my flat goes through, it's that or a lonely hotel room, so that would be lovely, thank you. Will it just be us?"

Charlotte placed her empty glass on the table and smirked. "It'll be a small gathering; Victoria will be at Natalie's house with Ben and his wife Julia, as well as their kids, Maya and Sam. Lou will be at the church, feeding the homeless people, Lizzie is going to Lanzarote with Bill for a bit of late winter sun, and Cathy is on a shift at the hospital. So, it'll just be the seven of us."

Ruth paused in putting her coat on. "Eh? Where do you get seven from?"

Charlotte laughed as they strolled through the crowded pub to the exit. She called over her shoulder at Ruth. "Oh, didn't I say? Mirabelle is hosting Biscuit, Tom, Molly and Peregrine, If the cat ladies can't be together at Christmas, then the bloody cats will!"

And both Ruthie and Charlotte left the pub in fits of hysterical laughter.

Chapter Fifty-Nine

Lou

After opening the lid and securely propping it up, Lou settled herself on the bench at the baby grand piano in the nave that sat in front of the choir section next to the chancel. She'd been practicing for a while and couldn't wait to play, except she was terrified of how the congregation might react to her unorthodox and secular choice of the prelude. Dear God! She could only hope they'd appreciate her selection and not decide she was unfit to continue serving them.

So here she was in the church, early, where she was the curate in training for full ministerial responsibilities. Christmas day had fallen on a Sunday this year, and her boss, Reverend Ellen, had asked her to conduct the service since she wanted to go to Hertfordshire to be with her family. "I have every faith in you," she'd said. "But don't be disappointed if not too many people show up. It'll be Christmas day, after all, and many people are out of town or getting ready for their feast."

Even prayer didn't help relieve the tightness in the pit of her stomach, and her collar felt scratchy. She began jiggling her knees up and down. This ought to be easy for an ex-actress, shouldn't it? After all, she was used to learning parts and playing roles, and she had practiced her sermon several times. She had the worship bulletins ready. Her traditional choice of carols throughout the service was sure to please everyone. Maybe she should just play "Joy to the World" for both the prelude and postlude.

Lou heard the church door open with its usual creak and looked up. She jumped off the bench and went down the aisle.

"Hello, my sweet," she said to Mac. "The service doesn't start for another thirty minutes, but you could help out with the luncheon we're preparing?"

As Mac kissed her cheek, she took his arm and escorted him to the fellowship hall where several church members were getting everything ready.

"Nervous?" he whispered as they walked.

"Terrified!" Lou replied and as she entered the hall, she looked around at the decorations and felt inordinately proud of these church folks wanting to give others a wonderful meal. The turkey and dressing smelled delicious; the gravy was staying hot on the warming plate; small plum puddings in the centre of each round table were flanked by colourful Christmas crackers.

After Lou greeted the volunteers with a warm smile, she introduced Mac, who'd stuck his hands in his pockets.

"Mac would love to help out. He's from Scotland. Perhaps he can mash the spuds and help serve people?"

Mac readily agreed. "Sure," he said.

"I'll get him an apron," one of the elders said. "Now, off you go, Vicar, and get ready for the masses."

Lou grinned at the pun knowing her congregant meant to be funny about them having masses of people show up. "Thank you all," she told the folks, noting the large punch bowl and hoping it was mainly ginger ale rather without any strong liquor. Some folks were trying to recover from alcoholism and attended AA.

She made her way to the pulpit and checked her sermon notes. All was in order. She was as ready as she was going to be. Except for the prelude. "Dear God," she muttered, "help, help, help," and went to sit at the piano.

At the last minute, people came rushing in to fill the pews. Their chattering stopped as she began to hit the keys. *God help me*, she silently pleaded, trying to stay calm.

"Love, love, love, love is all you need," rang out and she sang along, too busy looking at her music to pay attention to how anyone was responding. "All you need is love, all you need is love, all you need is love. Love, love! Love is all you need…" She glanced over her shoulder. "All you need is love. Everybody! All you need is love…"

A sense of warmth flooded her as people joined in and sang with her, "love, love, love, love is all you need."

At last, she played three keys in f-major to sound the end of the song, and she swung around to face the congregation. She immediately noticed Charlotte sitting with Ruth in a pew at the back.

"Thank you for bearing with my choice of music and thanks to John Lennon and Paul MacCartney. We will enjoy some traditional carols throughout our service. But let's begin with scripture read by our liturgist."

An elderly woman with silver hair stood up with an open Bible in her hands and read a passage about Mary and the birth of Jesus.

"Thanks, Susie," Lou said. "This is such a familiar story to most of us, but I'd like to emphasize the courage of Jesus's mother, Mary. Can you imagine—away from home with an old guy she hardly knew. She was fortunate he stuck with her even though she was already pregnant. Most men in those days wouldn't have given her the time of day. She would have been disgraced. But she was far from disgraced by having a baby."

Lou glanced around the sanctuary and smiled towards Victoria and her son Ben.

"Love is all you need," she sang. "We never hear about the difficulty of Mary's birth. It seems as if she must *poof* have birthed this baby without blood or labour pains. The Bible doesn't tell us much about the physicality of the birth, but it seems likely to me that Mary suffered. And even I, who've never been a mother, have seen, "Call the Midwives", and know it's painful and scary." Victoria nodded her head and started to cry. Ben put his arm around her shoulder and hugged her.

"Love is all you need," Lou sang out. "And Mary's courage to have this baby Jesus was a gift from God to all of humanity. Did you know there are at least four types of love mentioned in the Bible. There's eros for romantic love, storge for family love, philia for brotherly love, and agape for God's unconditional love. And all babies are gifts from God…"

Lou had plenty more to say but it was soon time for the prayers of the people. They bowed their heads and asked God to intercede for the needy, for the hurt, for the community, for the church and for peace in the world.

Finally, after more scripture readings interspersed with traditional carols, Lou sat at the piano and began the postlude:

Joy to the world, the Lord is come
Let earth receive her King
Let every heart prepare Him room
And heaven and nature sing
And heaven and nature sing
And heaven, and heaven and nature sing...

Lou stood up and thanked everyone for coming. "You are all invited to our luncheon, thanks to the love of our wonderful hospitality volunteers. May God bless you, everyone, and may God bless our lunch and our friendship with one another. And may God bless all mothers everywhere! Amen!"

Lou made her way to the fellowship hall, happy to see the tables occupied, and people in full swing bringing plates of food to everyone. Mac had taken off his apron and was pushing a cart of plates around, greeting everyone cordially.

"Mac," she sung, and hurried over to him, not worrying about how ministerial she was supposed to be, throwing her arms around him and giving him a big kiss.

After the hall emptied and everything was cleaned up, only Mac and Lou remained. "I have something I want to ask you, Louise," he said with a shy smile. "You don't know this about me, but I earned quite a lot of money during my time in Dubai, and I've decided to invest it in real estate. As you know, I already bought the B&B from Ruthie, but I can get a manager to run that for me. In fact, I'm buying a house nearby. The thing is," he said quietly, getting a small velvet box out of his coat pocket. "The thing is I thought I might move down here, and I'd like some company in my house."

Lou stared at the ring box in the palm of his big hand. Could it be what she thought it was? Her eyes widened as she watched him go down on his knees. "Louise, my darling Lou, I love you. Will you marry me?"

Chapter Sixty

Victoria

A fire blazed in Natalie's dining room, the logs crackling and spitting along to the Christmas music, chosen by the children: All I Want for Christmas, by Mariah Carey. The huge pine Christmas tree, decorated tastefully in red and gold, towered in the corner of the living room. There were dozens of neatly wrapped parcels underneath its boughs.

Until an hour later, with the beautiful wrap paper discarded into a pile ready for recycling, the children *oohing* and *aahing* over their new toys, and the adults smiling endearingly as they looked on.

At last, everyone took their seats at the table.

"Merry Christmas!" Victoria's heart warmed as the adults clinked their wine glasses and the two children, Maya and Sam, raised their cola cans in the air. The large oval dining table was covered with a pristine white tablecloth and decorated with lovely gold and red napkins. Victoria pushed aside her concerns about how long the tablecloth would stay pristine and brought herself back into the moment.

How wonderful this was. Sitting here with her son to the left of her, his wife beside him. Her granddaughter to her right, her grandson next to his sister. To think, this time last year, she had shared Christmas with Lizzie: a stilted, quiet affair as she acknowledged her romantic feelings toward her friend. A feeling she knew was never reciprocated, but now she was glad. Lizzie was happy with Bill; a good man who treated Lizzie with respect, and as his equal. She hoped they were having a wonderful time in Lanzarote.

Briefly she wondered how Lou was getting on after her first Christmas sermon. *Wow! What a turnaround that had been. Feisty, unconventional, sassy Lou, now a vicar!* She wondered how the relationship between Lou and Mac would evolve. She hoped it would thrive; Mac was a decent man, and Lou deserved to be loved, especially as Victoria now knew of the years of hurt Lou had been subjected to, waiting for an elusive and unattainable rat. It was almost surreal, but Victoria respected her for turning her life around.

Speaking of which, look at dear Charlotte; a woman she'd once considered a timid mouse; a walkover! Well look at her now! Assertive, driven and taking no nonsense from any man!

And then there was Cathy; once stuck in a rut with no drive, and no ambition, currently working a nursing shift at the hospital!

Gosh, they had all come full circle, since those dark wine-fuelled nights of book club. *And they never did finish that damn book!* She chuckled softly to herself, sipping her wine and saying a silent cheers to her friends: the Cat Ladies were awesome women who had taught her that life is too short for regret, that family and friends are everything, and to take brave jumps even when you're afraid.

She fleetingly wondered how her little Biscuit cat was getting on at Charlotte's. It was so kind that Charlotte had offered to take in all the cats whilst she was here, Lizzie was away, Lou was at church and Cathy was working. It was a good thing all the girls were neutered. *That bloody Peregrine was as sassy as his mother, Lou!* Victoria thought uncharitably.

"Pass the spuds, Sam." Ben's cheery voice interrupted her nostalgia, and Victoria smiled endearingly as her young grandson happily did his father's bidding.

"I'll do it, I'll do it!" Maya made a grab for the dish.

"Dad asked me!" Sam yelled, refusing to let go of the potatoes.

"Children!" Julia admonished, "if you drop those potatoes, I'll…"

Maya reluctantly let go of the dish and sat down with a grumpy *harumph* as Sam threw a smug smile in her direction.

Haha, yes, family! Victoria grinned at the kids. "Smells wonderful." she praised, her mouth genuinely watering at the divine smells and sights. "Thank you, Natalie. What a feast!" A huge, golden roasted turkey took pride of place in the centre of the table surrounded by dishes laden with crisp roast potatoes, countless vegetable dishes, as well as a jug of steaming gravy.

"You're all very welcome," Natalie smiled as everybody, even the children, murmured their appreciation for the delicious meal.

"It's so wonderful we're all together for Christmas," Julia, Ben's wife, stated solemnly, "I had begun to wonder if we might not..." She gulped as she choked back a sob and Ben grabbed her hand.

"It's okay," he said. "The point is, I *am* here, we *are* together, as family." He took Victoria's hand with his other one and squeezed gently. "All thanks to you," he smiled at her, and Victoria's eyes welled with tears.

"It's the least I could do," she whispered, wiping the tears away. "Now," she forced her mouth into a grin, "let's eat!"

"I'll drink to that!" cheered Natalie's partner, James, and they all raised their drinks again before tucking into the first of many delicious family Christmas dinners to come.

Epilogue

Biscuit

Biscuit, curled up on the sofa by the fire, opened a sleepy eye. *Gosh, that Mirabelle is such a tease! And that tailless Peregrine is falling for all her feline tricks! Typical Tomcat.* Biscuit rolled her eyes, stretched and curled back into herself. *The sooner Mum picks me up, the better,* she thought. She was happy Mum was with her new family today: she sensed her mum had softened over the last few months. She understood, because Mum had told her, Biscuit couldn't go with her for Christmas, what with Mum's son recently out of hospital and at risk of infection, and she was grateful for the lovely Charlotte lady. After all, she had just given them all generous servings of the turkey. She was just fed up with that Peregrine cat, sniffing the bottoms of the girls as he passed by, strutting his stuff like his bloody mother! Thank God her mum was so sensible. At least that wonky legged Tom – *very original name, Lizzie!* was as uninterested as she was in socialising. Biscuit stretched again, yawned and went off for another helping of turkey.

Mirabelle

"Oh Perry," Mirabelle purred, knowing her luxurious long hair was seductive. And being as polite as her mum, Charlotte, she resisted hissing and showing her claws. "Please stop," she meowed delicately. Peregrine's mum, Lou, always attracted the male species, but Mirabelle was not tempted by this pushy tailless cat. Although maybe she should take a lesson from her mum's book. Mum had changed so much recently; no longer wistfully gazing, talking to herself in the silence. These days she was busy with her new bestie Ruth and ignoring any calls from Colin or John. Mirabelle stood straight, placing her tail on the floor before Peregrine could sniff her bum again. "Stop now," she said, hissing and arching her back, causing Peregrine to turn and run. Yes, Mirabelle was just like her mum.

Tom

It took Tom a while to limp to the bowl of turkey that his mum's friend, Charlotte, had left for them all. That bloody Peregrine raced there and tried to butt him out of the way. He might be gimpy, but he was a match for any other tomcat. He had torn ears to show for it from when he'd competed with other alley cats. He was interested in Biscuit or Molly, but he didn't think they noticed him. Who would? He was only here because his mum had rescued him. They would have euthanized him otherwise at the stray animal home, what with his gammy leg and all. Bless his mum, Lizzie. He was truly grateful for her, and didn't blame her for jetting off with that Bill bloke. *He's alright, that Bill, and always gives me salmon treats.* Still, he'd be glad when his mum picked him up, he felt a little out of his comfort zone here in this way-too-clean-and-tidy house.

Molly

Molly edged in between Peregrine and Tom at the bowl of turkey. She would have preferred to stay curled up on her bed at home with Cathy, but she was hungry and thirsty. No way was she going to let those others get all the food and water. After snatching a big slice of turkey and backing away with it, she half-expected Tom or Peregrine to challenge her or worse. But Tom blocked Peregrine as if to protect her. Seriously, who did Peregrine think he was?

She wished her mum was here and when she'd put on her scrubs and put Molly in her cat carrier, she'd been a little scared, until she was dropped off at Charlotte's house with all these other cats. She'd smelled all of them on her mum before and wasn't scared of any of them. Plus, she knew Cathy would never run out on her or abandon her, especially now she worked in the hospital and had never been happier, sometimes picking her up and dancing around the kitchen with her.

Peregrine

Peregrine tried to sniff Mirabelle's behind again, but she turned on him with an evil glare. He might have viewed her resistance as a challenge, but he wasn't in the mood for a fight. Besides, there was always Biscuit or Molly.

He was much bigger and could easily defeat Tom and take Molly from him, except it looked as if Tom was a streetfighter. He stared at Tom's scarred head, giving him a low non-threatening growl to warn him to stay away. Peregrine did not want his fur ruffled.

Biscuit was a possibility for his amorous intentions except she was a rare ginger female, and he preferred to be the centre of attention, like his mum, Lou, who now wore long black robes and a white collar. She'd even stopped her bed behaviour, except when that Mac guy occasionally showed up. Really, unlike Mac, he didn't need any pussy and would have swished his tail, if he had one, to show his disdain for these felines.

As the cats lay about, satisfied from their turkey feast, Biscuit and Molly cuddled up together on the couch, Mirabelle lay stretched out on the carpeted stair leading up to the bedroom, Tom lay in front of the fire on his back, purring loudly, and Peregrine jumped onto the mantle, careful not to bat the knickknacks onto the floor. It was as if they'd been companions forever. Maybe it was a Christmas thing, peace on Earth and goodwill to all, but it was a bond of the best sort.

For these felines are loyal animals, and woe betide anybody who disrespects a cat or their ladies…

Also by the Authors
at
Rogue Phoenix Press

Ten Yen Tokyo

Seagull wanted to soar just like her namesake, didn't she? When she heads to Tokyo in search of herself, she is drawn into a world of mystery and miracles. Encountering many colourful characters as she travels, she is caught up in a dark underworld that forces her to question her scientific mind as well as her family values. Can Seagull believe in the unknown and can she lay the ghosts of her past to rest so that her future can begin?

Ten Yen True

Kaizen! That's what Caitlin, JJ, Paul, and Tommy need--to change for the better. When they each mysteriously receive one of four ten yen coins, none of them know or understand why or where their journey is about to take them.

Ten Yen True intertwines the lives of four people, all of whom have need of one another to bring about healing and wholeness and are being mysteriously helped by a Japanese monk. It is a story of hope, love, forgiveness and miracles, exploring the spiritual and psychological underpinnings of the main characters, demonstrating the interconnectedness of human beings.

About the Authors

Amanda Armstrong – Amanda lives with her cats in Kent, UK and this is her sixth work of fiction.

Christina St. Clair – Award winning author Christina lives with her cats in Kentucky, USA and has written articles, essays and fiction